What people are saying about *Ophelia's Oracle*:

"I would have given anything for a book like this growing up, especially in Jr. High School. I would have been a stronger person. It is the ultimate conversation betwe~~~ ~ ~~~~~~~ learning experiences. It's so easy to reference, with your highlight anytime. It's such a beautiful book. I'm just so emotional . . . ." –

"Ophelia's Oracle, by Donna DeNomme and Tina Proctor is a gift of following a young girl's journey of discovery, goddess myth and and creative." – *Cynthia James, Transformational Specialist, author o*

"This story of Ophelia is a beautiful and important work. It introduces young women to their power, beauty and relationship potential. It provides exercises that a mentor can use to encourage personal growth and spiritual development, and the story is told with an emotional sensitivity that makes it accessible to the little girl in us all." – *Luisah Teish, writer, storyteller, creative projects consultant, and founder of the School of Ancient Mysteries/Sacred Arts Center*

"What a joy to see this innovative combination of story, goddesses as role models, and personal growth exercises. Ophelia's Oracle creates an eye- and heart-opening look at new ways of being for young girls, which is both fun and useful. May it serve as a tool for transforming the lives of girls around the world—and their mothers! – *Deborah J. Grenn, Ph.D., Founder & Director, The Lilith Institute and author of* Lilith's Fire *and* Talking to Goddess

"What a beautiful book! Ophelia's Oracle is a gift of power, self-esteem, and light to any young woman." – *Fawn Germer, corporate speaker and best-selling author of* Hard Won Wisdom *and* Mustang Sallies.

"There is a scarcity of publications on this topic. There seems to be a taboo about speaking about mother/ daughter relationships when the girls are at this age. Many times the girls become distant, and there is a sacred silence between women about their struggles with their daughters. It often is just not talked about." – *Kathleen Biesadecki , nurse midwife and teacher, with thirty years experience working with mothers and daughters*

". . . fun and unique confidence-building ideas to bring awareness of inner wisdom, strength, and beauty." – *Debra Gano, award-winning author of* Beauty's Secret: A Girl's Discovery of Inner Beauty

"It's easy to let your friends tell you things and feel like you don't have anyone else to talk to. This book clearly shows the girls how to draw more strength from within them, to follow what they know in their heart." – *Brie Klein, mother of a teen girl*

"I really like the font. Cool font. Pictures are really amazing. Intriguing . . . " – *Heather Klein, age 13*

"Anybody who reads this book will be greatly enlightened. I love it! It's beautiful!" – *Joslin Graves, college student and singer/songwriter*

"I appreciate your simple way of accessing profound ideas." – *Sue Loving, former teacher/principal*

"From a true place of love, this book is: Joyful, Pure, Loving, Helpful, Appropriate, Gentle, and Empowering. For those becoming young women, and those who have completed more circles around the sun." – *Kathy Kaatz, Assistant Youth-Ministry Director*

Publisher: Inlightened Source Publishing
        18719 W. 60th Avenue
        Golden, CO 80403
        www.inlightenedsourcepublishing.com

LCCN: 2009931023

ISBN: 978-1-61539-958-1

Cover and interior design: Sue Lion
Illustrator: Sue Lion, www.suelionink.com
Additional illustrations: Rachelle Donahoe, www.rachelleart.com
Editor: Cara Cantarella

Printed in the U.S.A. by United Graphics Incorporated

"How Many Things I Can Be," by Kari Olman, reprinted with permission from *New Moon Magazine*; copyright New Moon Girl Media Inc., Duluth, MN. www.newmoon.com

"It's So Easy," lyrics from the CD, Now I Know, reprinted with permission from Cara Cantarella, www.caracantarella.com

"If I Were Brave," lyrics reprinted with permission from Jana Stanfield/Jimmy Scott, Jana StanTunes/English Channel Music (ASCAP), www.janastanfield.com

"The Nothing That We Are," lyrics from the CD, *The Scenic Route*, reprinted with permission from Erienne Romaine, www.erienneromaine.com

OPHELIA'S ORACLE

Donna DeNomme and Tina Proctor

Sue Lion, Illustrator

Acknowledgements

 When Donna and I decided to write an empowerment book for girls using goddess stories, we immediately went to a resort in Mexico for a week. We worked every morning writing ideas, discussing issues and choosing goddess stories that fit. We even entered a sand sculpture contest on the beach using a 12-year-old girl to be the body of the West African goddess, Yemaya. As we fashioned a beautiful mermaid tail around her, I told Yemaya's story to the contestants, and the judges gave us first prize! It was a magical beginning . . . and it took many years after that week to finally birth this book, but we found just the right people at just the right time to help make it happen.

We can't imagine any illustrator and book designer as imaginative, good-natured, and creative as Sue Lion. Whenever we had a problem or issue, we would sit by her computer and hear her say, "Watch this!" as something beautiful appeared. She was truly our partner in every way. She not only created six original art pieces but found places for all of the girls' art, poetry, and sayings, that just made them "pop." Rachelle Donahoe's vibrantly colored messages also added a spark to several of the pages.

Cara Cantarella, who agreed to be our editor after hearing Donna read parts of the book to her, was so helpful and supportive. We appreciated the little clouds next to paragraphs that said "I love this!" A special thanks to Jeniffer Thompson, author of *Web Site Wow*, who suggested that we include a fictional character. Thus, Ophelia was born, and we can't wait to see what she does in the next book in the series!

I would like to thank my wisdom teachers and sister scholars at New College of California, who helped me reach deep inside to find and believe in that creative spark which has finally come into form. I offer much gratitude to my mother, Betty Proctor, who filled my life with books, authors, and a love of reading. To Jane Grogan, my mother-in-law, I deeply honor our connection through the goddess and appreciate the many classes we taught together about goddess history and myth. A very special thanks to my husband and soul mate, Dennis, for his ideas and his understanding of middle school kids! My children, Kelley, Tyler, and Dylan, have all been an inspiration in their own challenges and growth. Thanks for all their encouragement and for NEVER once saying, "Are you ever going to finish this book?"

Tina

July 2009

Dianne Jenett, when we were inspired to ask you to write our Foreword, we did not realize just how much your beautiful words would be the perfect blessing. As the new baby is held in the loving arms of a wise godmother, your presence holds us up. We are now ready to step out!

On a personal note, I would like to thank my father, George DeNomme, who instilled in me a strong belief in myself and my abilities, and my mother, Pauline Schulte, who showed me the importance of family and of community. To Darcey, Doreen, Darris, Darryl, Mike, Lori, Wayne, and Sue, my siblings, the lessons are too numerous to mention! To my Uncle Hank and Aunt Kathy, your love and understanding means the world to me. To my goddaughter, Kayla Farwell, who was born in China, may you always know who you are . . . . Todd and Jessica, I love you.

And how do I thank Dianne Fresquez, who has opened my eyes in so many ways? Dianne was the initial inspiration for Ophelia, as I was privy to Dianne's journey of understanding her own mixed cultural heritage. Some of the names of our characters are borrowed from Dianne's family. As the owner of For Heaven's Sake Bookstore and Events Center, Dianne never missed an opportunity to promote our work, or to offer us workshop space with the girls. And a little "secret" is that a few of Ophelia's best lines originate with our youthful Dianne!

Tina and Sue, thank you for your wisdom and patience. I appreciate that we all share the wonder of truth expressing through many channels. Working with you both has been a beautiful journey; one which carries on into the horizon.

To all of those who have supported me through the past several years with my first book, *Turtle Wisdom: Coming Home to Yourself*, thank you. As I contact industry professionals to launch *Ophelia's Oracle*, I am reminded just how important personal relationships are. Thank you for warm response as we pass along the first of many, many books in our girls series.

Tina and I taught years of classes, workshops, and focus groups in preparation for this book. To all the parents, we offer our heartfelt appreciation for your trust—sharing your most precious gift with us, your girls. To all the girls, those we have worked with and those we have yet to meet, remember that you hold the brightness of the future!

Love and blessings,

Donna
July 2009

Foreword

Ophelia's Oracle is an exquisite cup overflowing with stories of the divine feminine which mothers and grandmothers have told to their daughters in many parts of the world. The timeless wisdom in these stories connects girls to the past and gives them resources and tools they need to become the capable and compassionate women our world needs. Girls and women of all ages can be inspired by the ancient stories told so lovingly in this book.

Over the past ten years as a director of a Woman's Spirituality Masters Program, I've had the privilege of witnessing the deep changes women experience when they are introduced to the divine feminine and begin to understand they are part of a historical past in which women were and are sacred. Tina, already an accomplished storyteller when she came into our program, immediately understood the power of the goddess stories and, in collaboration with Donna, began working on ways they could make them accessible to girls who are on the brink of womanhood. When I opened the first chapter I experienced delight in the beauty of the book and deep joy that their years of research and collaboration had gifted us with *Ophelia's Oracle*.

The authors have skillfully designed activities and exercises using creative expression, meditation, and self-reflection to guide the girls to search inside themselves for answers and to tap into their own internal wisdom and authority. The lively and lush illustrations and drawings invite girls to engage their own imagination and creative forces. Real stories model the ways empowered girls can work on behalf of their communities.

Ophelia's Oracle is a cup which can be passed from woman to woman, girl to girl, as a sign of sisterhood and as an ever-filling source of inspiration and wisdom.

Dianne Jenett, Ph.D

Co-director, Women's Spirituality Masters Program
Institute of Transpersonal Psychology
Palo Alto, California

Portals are doorways
To a place of new adventures

You are about to enter
Five portals of story and fun

1 • Who is that Girl in the Mirror

2 • Believing in Yourself

3 • The Power of One

4 • Free to Be Me

5 • The Winds of Change

Enter with joy and anticipation

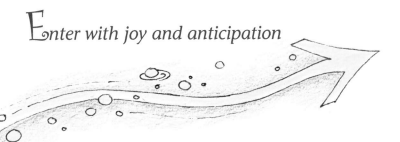

Who is That Girl in the Mirror?

Ophelia leaned on the strength of her forearms, her head pivoted at an angle, as she scrutinized the reflection in the mirror . . . . "Who am I?" she mused. "WHAT am I?"

As she looked at every detail of the shape and color of her face, she had to admit it. "I am good looking!" she said out loud to no one but herself.

"But who am I? What am I? Where do I fit in?"

These thoughts might be the typical pondering of any twelve-year-old girl, and yet for Ophelia, it was a bit more complicated. Her family was multi-cultural, making it difficult for this girl to know exactly where she fit in. She stared at the beautiful dark almond eyes of her mother, who was Japanese. Her father's mother was from Mexico, and his father was born and raised in the U.S., like Ophelia herself. She loved her parents and they were very good to her, but their blended heritage confused her. Once in a while someone asked her, "Where did you come from?" and that wasn't too bad, although sometimes it could be embarrassing because honestly Ophelia didn't know how to answer that question—not really. The boys from the apartment building down the street taunted her and called her names, saying she wasn't even an American. Ophelia knew she was American, yet she wasn't certain if she really belonged . . . .

Today was a special day in her household. Her grandmother was coming for a six-week visit from Japan. It had been many years since Ophelia had seen Obachan Chiyo. She just called her Obachan, which means grandmother, and she remembered her as a beautiful woman, with a strength about her that was quite different from anyone else she knew. Obachan's strength was quiet in nature, but she was always able to get her point across in such a way that made things happen. Ophelia was only eight when Chiyo had last journeyed from Japan to visit her only daughter and her family. Ophelia was expectantly awaiting her grandmother's arrival in less than an hour. This was the catalyst for her mirror musings. What would Obachan see in her face? She had grown so much in the last four years, and her face had changed shape. Would her dear Obachan recognize her? Ophelia was not fully Japanese and yet she could distinctly see that influence in her eyes and her face.

"I hope I look okay for her . . . ," she thought as she finished dressing and joined the rest of the family at the breakfast table.

"Good morning, Mom, Dad," she said as she gave her little brother a poke on the way to her seat on the breakfast bench. Nine-year-old Mateo was sometimes a pest, but he wasn't too bad, as brothers go.

"I wish I could have butterscotch pudding for breakfast this morning," she said.

"Oh, Ophelia," her mother groaned in that I-just-don't-believe-you tone.

"Could I?" Opehlia asked again.

"No, you most certainly cannot."

"But I never get to eat butterscotch pudding," she complained.

"You just had some for dinner last night," her mother responded with one hand on her hip.

"Well, not in massive quantities . . . . It's my favorite!"

"We'll have blueberry pancakes tomorrow morning once Obachan is here. For now, just get yourself some cereal. We need to leave for the airport soon. Did you change the sheets in the guest room like I asked you?"

"Yes, Mama," Ophelia answered, "and I cut some fresh roses from the garden for her room, too."

"What a lovely idea, Ophelia. Your grandmother helped me plant that rose bush the last time she was here."

After breakfast, Ophelia grabbed her phone from her bedroom, glancing at it as she headed down the hallway. She bent down to fiddle with her shoe. She was really responding to a text from her best friend Marissa, who had asked, "Where r u?"

"Going 2 airport 2 get Obachan."

"U will miss pizza party."

"I know. C u later."

"Ophelia," her mother called as she waited in the car. "I'm coming, Mama. I just had to tie my shoe," Ophelia answered, knowing that her mother sometimes criticized the amount of time she spent texting.

The next few days were filled with many family activities, most of which were fun for Ophelia. It was a joyful time of reconnecting with her grandmother. Things had always been easy between the two of them—quite different than it was with Ophelia and her mother. She loved her mother dearly, but sometimes their interactions were strained, and after all, her mother was "the boss." Ophelia knew Obachan adored her, and her grandmother had a way of setting her straight without ever seeming like she was scolding or being bossy. Ophelia adored her Obachan, too!

On the third day, Chiyo welcomed the opportunity to spend the entire day with her only granddaughter. My, Ophelia had grown so much in the four years since they had been together. Anything they would have done would have been special, but on this particular day, she thought it was simply glorious to be strolling through the Botanic Gardens, not yet quite in the peak of their growth. Everything was somewhat new with the late spring budding. Tulips in an array of colors lined the path and reached upward toward the warm noonday sun. Chiyo loved it here with her granddaughter's hand in hers. Ophelia-chan's energy always made her smile with gratitude.

Together Ophelia and Chiyo wove through the garden paths admiring the flowers, the bushes, and the trees all tended with great care. Pots and containers were strategically placed in a striking design of form and color. Even the rocks held a place of importance in the grand scheme of this place. The two found themselves near a giant weeping willow tree, which stood with its flexible strength overlooking the serene water of the pond beneath. Ducks and geese paddled in the water and an elegant blue heron stood motionlessly watching for small fish to swim by.

Chiyo led Ophelia to a bench underneath the willow tree. The branches danced in the breeze, as the two sat sheltered in this cozy spot.

"Obachan, tell me more about Japan," Ophelia requested.

"Ophelia-chan, let me tell you the story of Amaterasu," Chiyo responded with a knowing smile.

"In Japan," Chiyo began, "Amaterasu watches over all the Earth, guiding the building of irrigation canals, nurturing the fields of growing rice, and overseeing her palace in the great Weaving Hall of Heaven. As the sun goddess, she is known as 'The Great Woman Who Possesses Noon.'"

"Her brother, Susanowo, is god of the oceans, but is often unhappy and jealous because he imagines that Amaterasu has the greater power. Once he traveled to see her, and she suspected that he was going to challenge her in some way. But when she asked him directly, he denied he had any such intention. She wanted to believe her younger brother, for she wished for a closer relationship." At the mention of a younger brother, Ophelia began to listen intently.

"Yet not long after that," Chiyo continued, "Susanowo blocked the canals of irrigation that are so important to the people. He piled them with mounds of dirt so that the waters could no longer flow to the thirsty plants. Like a spoiled child, he entered the places where rice plants grew and stomped upon each plant until the rice paddies lay in muddy chaos. As if he had not already caused enough destruction, he smeared the weaving hall in the palace of the goddess with the excrement of animals and humans. The smell was atrocious and it took many days of scrubbing to get it all clean."

Amaterasu (Ah mah ter AH sue)

Susanowo (Sue shaw NO woe)

Uzume (Oo ZOO may)

"Yuck, how could she stand it?" Ophelia wrinkled her nose in disgust.

"Patiently, Amaterasu forgave him by saying he had swallowed too much sake wine, which he often drank with his friends. But even then Susanowo wasn't finished. He murdered a colt and heaved its body into the weaving house. As the weight of the horse struck the looms and tables of the hall, they fell upon the women who were weaving the tapestries, sending several to the Land of the Dead.

"This time Amaterasu became enraged at his behavior," Chiyo increased her volume and puffed out her chest. "How dare he treat her and the women who work with her that way? Did he think he could pick a fight? Did he think that he would win a fight and then have more power?

"Amaterasu was filled with anger, but she refused to fight on such a demeaning level. So she announced her rage by withdrawing her warmth and the light that brought the goodness of life. She entered the Cave of Heaven, and pulled the great door shut behind her. No longer was there day and night. No longer did the golden light help the rice to grow. Life was impossible. The gods and goddesses of heaven met together outside the cave to discuss what might be done to restore the treasured presence of the sun goddess. First they decreed that Susanowo would be punished and fined, and then they banished him from the heavens. But they did not know how to tempt Amaterasu from her cave, or how to let her know that her brother had been sent away.

"Do you know what they did next, Ophelia-chan? Chiyo asked with a smile. "They invited the playful goddess, Uzume, to dance by the entrance of the cave, making motions and faces that would bring such laughter from those who watched her. Her wild and bawdy dance continued, as she took off articles of clothing and caused uproarious laughter.

"Amaterasu was so intrigued by the wild laughter outside the cave that she opened the door a crack and found herself facing the mirror that had been hung upon the sacred Sakaki tree. So intense was the brilliant image, and so beautiful (for she had never seen her reflection before), that she stepped out to take a closer look. The others quickly grabbed the door and pulled it open. With a rope, they tied the cave's rock door open so it could never be closed so tightly again. Thus, the life-sustaining light of the sun returned to bring warmth and joy to the Earth."

Nicola, age 10

Who Is That Girl in the Mirror?

"So, my granddaughter," Chiyo looked into Ophelia's dark eyes, "Amaterasu recognized that her beauty and strength were magnificent."

"Obachan," Ophelia said, "I love that story. Will you tell it to me again sometime? Amaterasu is a brave and beautiful woman."

"Certainly she is," Chiyo said. "Amaterasu is a goddess who claimed her full power when she saw the beauty of her own reflection in the mirror. By realizing her true value, she became 'The Woman Who Possesses Noon'— the highest and fullest point of the sun. She is an example for all of us to realize the fullness of our potential.

"Her eight-sided mirror is kept in the Great Shrine at Ise, Japan where it rests in a series of boxes and brocade bags that have been added over the more than 1,500 years of the shrine's history. Perhaps we will visit there someday, for I like to think of Amaterasu as one of our ancestors, too."

Ophelia and her Obachan stood up from the bench, again holding hands as they headed toward the little café in the corner of the gardens.

Things that might remind you of Amaterasu:

Large red candle

Japanese flag

Mirror

Amaterasu card from goddess card deck

    Go to www.opheliasoracle.com to see our favorites!

Amaterasu picture from Internet

Red cloth or Japanese fabric

Bowl of rice, chopsticks

Sun

CHAPTER 1

Discovering the Real You

Mirror, Mirror on the Wall

Do you ever take the time to sit and be still? Sit in a quiet place without lots of distractions. Take some time to listen to your own thoughts and feel your own feelings. Let go of anyone else's expectations and just hang with yourself! Let go of your day and anything that happened to you today. Open to what pops into your mind and what feelings you get in your body. There is no goal in this type of contemplative meditation other than to spend some quality time just with you. Whatever your experience, it is right.

Another variation of this meditation can be to spend some time looking at your reflection in the mirror. Like Ophelia, think about who you are—what do you see? What do you notice about the girl who looks back at you? Be aware of the tone of your words with yourself—are they accepting or critical?

Inner Mirror Reflection

In the following exercise, we will ask you to meditate on a specific question or questions. Do not put a lot of effort into figuring it out. There is no right or wrong answer. Simply allow the thoughts and feelings to surface naturally, as you see whatever it is that is appropriate at this time. If you have never followed a guided meditation before, try this process a few times to give it a chance. You may be surprised at what you discover about yourself!

You can also partner up with a friend and read these words to each other. Or you can have your parent or another adult prompt you with the questions. You can also go to our website at www.opheliasoracle.com to download this meditation to your computer or iPod.

Shayna, age 14

In your inner imagination, your "mind's eye," envision a beautiful, eight-sided mirror. This is a Japanese Shinto mirror. If you can actually see a picture of the eight-sided mirror, that is good. If you do not see a picture in your mind, that's okay too—simply imagine it to be there . . . .

Now look into that imaginary mirror and see your own reflection. Look into your own eyes . . . .

Watch yourself joining your hands together at heart level, with your fingers pointed upward in a respectful, Japanese prayer position. Bow slightly forward as you show a reverence for this time of true self-reflection.

Return again to look intently at your image in this inner mirror. Notice your thoughts and reactions to seeing your reflection:

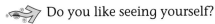 Do you like seeing yourself?

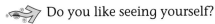 Do you like the face looking back? Or do you feel uncomfortable?

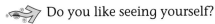 Do you remember how other people have complimented you on your appearance?

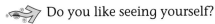 Do you hear inner criticism about the way you look?

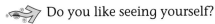 Do you remember other people's negative comments about your physical appearance?

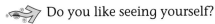 Do you focus on the things you do not like about the way you look?

Carly, age 10

Who Is That Girl in the Mirror?

Look beyond the physical . . . still gazing in your own eyes, look deeper into yourself. Move within—into a sense of your personality and character. Allow your mind to wander, as you reflect on your way of being in the world. Consider one or more of the following questions:

- How do you live in the world?
- What kind of person are you? How do you treat others? How do you treat yourself?
- What qualities do you appreciate about yourself?

Imagine yourself having a sun source at your heart center, which radiates out and touches all you meet. How do your rays impact the world? Are there things about yourself that you would like to change? Remember, you are not looking at life situations here, like events that you would like to change or experiences that you would like to have happen to you. You are focusing on qualities—your character; your true nature.

- Are you expressing who you are on the inside to the outside world?
- Do you share your true being or pretend to be something other than who you truly are?
    (We all wear many faces and play various roles, so it is okay to have many sides to your personality.)
- Are the inner and outer aspects of you in sync?
- Are your thoughts or feelings in your inner world in disagreement with how you appear in the outer world?

What is your true nature? Are there times when you fail to shine your inner light, but instead keep it clouded over and hidden inside of you?

This "inner mirror of the imagination" is a non-judgmental mirror, so in your exploration, try to look at yourself openly and objectively with as much understanding as possible. Look at yourself with curiosity and interest, as if you are about to discover a big secret! If critical or self-defeating thoughts come in, thank them for sharing, but then let them go. It is better not to dwell here, as these thoughts are unproductive. Acceptance of yourself can lead to change, if you desire, in a much better way.

Observe your feelings. Again, do not judge your feelings as good or bad, but simply note them. Allow these feelings to come up and be expressed appropriately. If the process makes you angry, then feel angry. Later, you can ask yourself why that feeling might have surfaced for you. What part of this exploration triggered anger? If you feel sad, let yourself cry, and cry until you are done. Allow yourself to be sad. If you are joyful or exhilarated, then express that. This is an important part of this process—feeling your emotions, honoring them as a valuable part of your expression, and then giving them space to be. Allowing these emotions helps you to honor and respect yourself.

If any of your feelings are overwhelming or confusing, talk with a helpful, trustworthy adult to share and discuss your feelings. Make sure you ask for help if you need it.

Come back to center. Focus on the simple act of your breath—flowing in and then out—to relax you once again and to help quiet your mind.

Who Is That Girl in the Mirror?

Now return to the stillness. Just breathe. Let go of any task or thought and just breathe. Allow the breath to release any difficult thoughts or emotions that may have surfaced. Let them float out with the breath. Imagine your breath emptying you of any burdens or difficulties from this inner search. Let the difficulties flow out with each breath . . . . imagine you are being filled with vital life force energy on the in-breath. Filled and recharged with positive energy. You are refreshed and renewed!

Thank yourself for participating so fully in this process. Imagine yourself bowing once more in the Japanese prayer position, as a sign of respect to the goddess Amaterasu, and to yourself . . . . One more conscious breath to seal this special time . . . . and gently open your eyes.

You may want to peek at yourself in a mirror to notice if there has been any change in your physical appearance—in your reflection—during this process.

You may also want to jot a few notes if anything important came up for you. It may also take several times to reflect on all that was presented here. Pick and choose what works for you.

This is your special time
to get to know your own inner reflection!

Inner Reflection Summary:

✳ Close your eyes and look inside an inner mirror.

✳ Imagine yourself looking into your own eyes.

✳ Go beyond the physical and examine your personality, your character.

✳ Are there parts of your outer expression that conflict with your inner reality?

✳ Examine your experience.

✳ Observe your feelings.

✳ Come back to center. Release your thoughts and feelings. Breathe . . . empty out and recharge with life energy. Ahh!

✳ Thank Amaterasu and thank yourself.

Ophelia awoke on Saturday with much anticipation for the day ahead. She had plans with her friend, Jenna. The girls were going to draw together. They were working on an art project and found that when they got together, their drawing somehow came more easily. There was something about the camarederie of sharing a creative space that seemed to make each of them better artists, even though they were working on solo pieces.

At the first light of the new day, Ophelia bounded out of bed and searched on her shelf for her masterpiece in process.

"Where is it?" she said out loud, beginning to worry a bit, for she was certain that she had put her canvas right there on the shelf with her art supplies. She searched every shelf, moving with more determination as each stagnant nook was void of the vibrant colors she remembered gracing her self-portrait.

Who Is That Girl in the Mirror?

That had been the assignment—draw or paint something that captured your essence. Not just your physical appearance, but your personality, and even more than that, who you were at your innermost character. Ophelia was surprised at how the task had consumed her and how she tirelessly pursued it. With all of her mirror musings lately, this was a personal mission for her—to discover who she truly was and how she showed herself to others. Obachan being here always got her thinking in different ways, and the girl saw the art assignment as an opportunity to explore the many possibilities that she was discovering about herself. She was pleased with what it had brought up so far, and the painting gave her a strange sense of satisfaction. So, now where was it? Feeling as if she was someone who had buried a great treasure and returned only to find it gone, Ophelia felt her determination turn into frustration.

"Where is it?" She said again, even more determined. Standing with her hands on her hips, she let out a heavy sigh, which sounded more like a growl. She was beginning to get a funny feeling.

The hem of the comforter draped over her bed seemed inviting as it lay cross-wise, where it had been kicked off in the warm spring night by her feet seeking freedom. Ophelia dove to the floor, stretching as she pulled out her missing canvas, only to see that there was a dark handprint on the side of the portrait and that pieces of the colorful paint had been chipped away. Shock and dismay bled into sheer anger at the violation.

MATT – TAY – OH, she yelled at the top of her voice, as she ran into the hall in search of her brother . . . .

Dealing with Anger

Have you ever been so angry at someone that you wanted to scream at them or physically hurt them? Have you ever caused harm to someone and were sorry about it later? The story of Amaterasu demonstrates how effective it can be to retreat during a time of anger instead of lashing out and hurting another person. After being alone with her anger, Amaterasu was enticed to look at a mirror and see deeper into the essence of who she really was.

"When I get angry at the world, I go to my special private place and just sit until the anger goes away," said Jamie, a girl in one of our goddess classes. When she heard the story of Amaterasu, she immediately understood the need for private, alone time to feel the anger, let it disappear, and invite the calm to return.

We all get angry at times, at our parents, friends, "the world," or ourselves. Sometimes the anger is based on being hurt or disappointed. Sometimes you may think your parents just expect too much of you or that a friend is being disloyal.

Some girls said that when they get angry, they lash out at someone else, or they tease the dog. Their anger is not directed at the person who made them angry. The full blast of the feeling is instead directed at a little brother or sister or someone else who is an easy target for their emotion.

What do you do when you get angry?

Think for a few minutes about the following ideas. If you have a small notebook or journal, you may want to write down your thoughts. They are only for YOU to see and think about, so be honest and thorough in your responses.

> Who am I angry with right now or sometime in the past? Or what situation makes me angry?

> Why am I angry with this person or situation?

Recognizing that you ARE angry is the first step to resolution!

Some girls are told by their parents or teachers not to be angry—that it isn't acceptable for females. Anger is a "bad" emotion compared to a "good" emotion like happiness. Remember that every emotion you feel is honest and real. As humans, all of us get angry occasionally. We may even get furious and feel full of rage. No one can go through life without these feelings, because anger is a healthy biological experience.

Q: What causes the tides in the oceans?

A. The tides are a fight between the Earth and the Moon. All water tends to flow towards the moon, because there is no water on the moon, and nature hates a vacuum. I forget where the sun joins in this fight.

(Answer on a science exam!)

"He who smiles rather than rages is always the stronger."

Japanese wisdom

When I get angry, what do I do about it?

When can I appropriately let my anger out?

What can I do that isn't destructive?

Remember that every emotion you feel is real.

When experiencing your emotions, it is helpful to acknowledge them (at least to yourself, if not to others). Allow yourself to feel them, and then if you choose, try to shift them by working them through.

Here are some ideas for turning that explosive anger into peaceful calm, or releasing that simmering anger into the air and inviting a sense of joyful relief, in spite of whatever may have triggered your emotions.

✳ Scream into a pillow until you are tired of doing it. Then sit quietly and say, "I release this anger so that it can't hurt me or anyone else."

✳ Put your anger into a journal and then rip up the pages. Tell yourself that when you finish ripping, the anger will be gone.

✳ Put on your favorite dance music and move through your anger. Moving your body to a beat is a great way to physically release the anger.

✳ Build a nest with blankets and pillows and tell yourself out loud why you are mad. When you are finished talking, cuddle with the pillows and let the anger release.

✳ Seek out a friend or an adult who can help by just listening as you talk about how you feel. We all need people who can allow us to vent our feelings without judging us or trying to "fix" how we feel.

Sometimes, it takes time to work the anger through. You may not be able to release it with one of these techniques, but instead may need to observe it, experience it, and ask for help in working it through. Trust the process and trust in your ability to find your way to a calmer place.

Sometimes anger is a "false face" for another true emotion that is underneath it. You may want to contemplate whether your anger is covering up feelings of insecurity, fear, confusion, or hurt.

Be careful not to fall into a rut of anger where you walk around with a constant "chip on your shoulder." If this sounds like you, again ask for help. Life is too short to see it through the cloudy lens of discontent.

When you get angry, sometimes the best way to feel better is to do something that can help the very situation that made you angry. While working on this chapter, we (the authors) "lost" our changes! When we discovered they were gone, we channeled our disappointment and anger into recreating our work.

The trick is to figure out what to do with anger instead of causing harm to yourself or someone else.

sometimes, she cries and has BIG, SLOPPY emotions ...

and it's okay.

Air Conditioning

Think about the person or situation you are currently angry with or have felt angry with in the past.

Do you feel the anger in your body? Is it a headache? Does your stomach hurt? Does your lower back ache? Do you breathe more quickly? Where in your body do you hold anger? Do you hold it in the same place each time you are angry? Do you "store it?" It is helpful to realize how your body reacts to the emotion of anger. You can allow the natural response of anger without keeping it held in your body for any length of time. Stored anger over time can have negative physical effects.

Here is a useful way to release angry thoughts and feelings from your body: Close your eyes and take several deep breaths. As you breathe the fresh air in, think of yourself as an air conditioner. The fresh air replaces the stale, angry air.

As you breathe out, let the anger go with it. Breathe fresh air in and breathe out any angry feelings that may be stuck inside. If you feel the anger in a place in your body, such as your lower back, imagine the fresh air going to that place. Then let the stale air release from there and leave your body through your lungs. Breathe deeply for a few minutes as you imagine the air conditioner working through your lungs.

"My boyfriend got jumped after school and then
he wanted to go back and hit them. It took all of his energy not to . . .
and I said to him, "Breathe. Just breathe." Anonymous, age 12

Who Is That Girl in the Mirror?

It is important to be aware of your body and the emotions that you might bury there . . . and to find ways to release them appropriately. Engaging in a physical activity, like playing ball or going for a run, can help with this letting go process, too.

> By recognizing that you have choices around anger, anger becomes your friend. You don't have to be so afraid of it.

You can probably think of more ways to change your anger into calm and even to allow yourself to be happy. Having ideas about what to do when you feel angry will help you through difficult times in the years ahead. There may be times where you just allow yourself to feel angry. Perhaps when it is for a good reason, simply being angry may be a healthy process. Later, if your anger does not resolve itself naturally, you can revisit the situation and work through it.

> Knowing what to do with your anger
> is responsible and empowering!

Knowing what to do with anger makes me feel.....

Power

like I have power.

Shayna, age 12

"MAT – TAY – OH," Ophelia heard her voice reverberating as it bounced off the hallway walls, meandering into the far reaches of her home. Her brother was nowhere in sight. She glanced inside the open doorway of Mat's room, the damaged canvas dangling at her side . . . .

Obachan Chiyo met her in the hallway, looking with kindness on the obviously distraught girl. She spoke gently with the poignant power of a single comforting word, "Amaterasu." Her grandmother disappeared back into the study, leaving Ophelia standing alone with her canvas in one hand and her anger in the other.

"What would Amaterasu do?" she thought.

Ophelia slipped out the back door and took refuge in the little garden her mother had planted in the backyard. She sat on a deep, multi-colored red rock with tiny patterns of granite throughout. This was the one that she had helped her mother choose from the landscape yard, where all you could see were boulders and rocks of all sizes, shapes, and colors. This one had seemed special somehow to Ophelia, and she loved it from the moment they met!

Now she found refuge sitting on the sturdy rock, overlooking the koi fish, swimming unencumbered in the small pond. She noticed that the water lilies were on the verge of opening and she remembered how last year she had loved to just sit and soak in the beauty of the lilies. One time she had watched for so long that she had actually seen one lily in motion, stretching its delicate arms wide. Ophelia breathed in the fragrant scents of the awakening garden with every breath, and with every breath her body relaxed a little more.

Who Is That Girl in the Mirror?

After what seemed like a long time but what had probably only been about fifteen minutes, Ophelia reluctantly surveyed her invaded canvas. She realized that the paint chips could easily be touched up with new paint. In the light of the emerging day, softened by the shade of the locust tree, she noticed an interesting pattern in the smudged hand print. Ophelia dashed for her paints as she realized that she could incorporate the offensive print into the unfolding tapestry of her painting.

"It'll work," she mused as she reached for the oils.

Our Connection to All Things

Amaterasu is the Shinto Sun Goddess of Japan. The current emperor, Akihito, is the 125th emperor of Japan, one of a long line of rulers who consider themselves descendants of Amaterasu. Shinto is uniquely Japanese. Unlike Christianity and Buddhism, it is a practice which evolved with the development of Japanese society through practice and rituals. There are no sacred writings, rules or commands. Shinto supports personal experience rather than writings or sacred principles.

Shinto practitioners believe that nature and all life are to be respected. In Shinto, kami is the divine essence of the natural world. Trees, rocks, flowers, animals, rivers, and people hold the spirit of kami (kah me).

Try this with your family:

✳ Take a bowl of uncooked rice and pass it around the table.

✳ Say: I give thanks to _____ (the farmers, the Earth, Spirit, God, Goddess, or whatever name is meaningful for your family) for providing the food for this meal, the sunshine which grows all our food, the animals which have given us _____ (this steak, this fish, etc.) the plants which have given us this salad or these vegetables, and the grain which has been used to make the bread, etc.

✳ Honor the kami which comes in many forms!

✳ Have each person say something in gratitude and then pass the bowl. Keep the bowl on the table during your meal as a reminder of all of the blessings you share.

We are all related

Have you seen pictures of a Japanese garden with sand, rocks, and trees laid out in a simple pattern? All of these elements of the garden, both living and non-living, possess kami. The spiritual quality of the garden gives the Shinto practitioner a feeling of peace and a sense of connection to the divine spirit in nature.

Madison, age 12

Have you ever felt your troubles or tension melt away when you are in a natural setting, such as a park, or on a trail, or by a stream? Or perhaps even in your own backyard, like Ophelia? Being in a quiet outdoor place can bring a sense of connection and acceptance. Try sitting or walking outside, away from the traffic and noise of your community, and imagine your kami connected to the kami of all the other elements of the place you have chosen. Is there a special rock or log to sit on? Can you hear the birds, the wind, and the sound of water? Whether you live near desert, forest, or prairie, all of these places have special healing qualities.

Having a connection to a certain species of wildlife or to a tree can also bring a sense that you are not alone. Is there an animal or bird that appears in your dreams? Do you have a favorite creature that you like to read or watch television shows about?

Sometimes we see animals up close when we sit quietly outdoors for a period of time. Perhaps a bird will come close, hoping for a hand-out of food. A squirrel or a lizard may appear if he doesn't see your body moving. You may have the opportunity to see a deer or a fox, for even these animals appear in both rural and urban set-tings. A willow tree or a large oak that you can climb and sit in may also create your kami connection.

Tina had an experience with a group of three squid which changed her views about squid, bringing a great appreciation and affection for these animals. She was snorkeling in warm, shallow waters off the coast of Mexico, when three tiny squid approached her and stayed just beyond her reach. The creatures were about six inches long swimming in tight formation. They stopped to look at her, and as she slowly moved her head around, the squid also moved—so they were always in her line of sight. If she moved her body backwards, they would move toward her. If she moved to the side, so would they. For several minutes they did this dance of wonder and curiosity. It was a magical moment of

Who Is That Girl in the Mirror?

inter-species communication that Tina will never forget. And because of that chance encounter, Tina has never eaten calamari (squid) again!

If you can't get outdoors right now, you can look through magazines or on the Internet for pictures of your favorite animal. It may be an animal or bird that you have never seen in the wild, such as an eagle or elephant or monkey. Think about the qualities the animal has that you admire or appreciate. Does it have strength and power like a tiger, grace and intelligence like a raven, or the playfulness and agility of an otter? These are qualities that you can find inside yourself. Remember your kami connection and know that you can continue to develop the qualities you observe and admire in nature.

In cultures that live close to the earth, many people believe they have totem animals that protect them and help them in times of need. These may be fish, insects such as butterflies, or even plants. Sometimes animals that appear in your dreams or in your imagination when you are awake can serve as your totem guides. They are always helpful and not threatening. Some cultures believe you have one totem animal your whole life, while others feel that different animals serve as protectors at different times. And remember, a dragonfly is just as powerful as a bear for a totem. Each plant or animal has much to teach us . . . these are qualities that you can find inside yourself.

Remember your kami connection
and know that you can continue to develop
the qualities you admire.

deer

Aspen, age 7

Many goddesses have animals associated with them. The deer is sacred to Artemis, a Greek goddess, who could run swiftly through the forest and was seen as the protector of women and animals. Changing Woman, a Navajo and Apache goddess who represents the various stages of a woman's life, is often shown with a snake, an animal that sheds its skin and therefore symbolizes transformation. Saraswati, the Hindu goddess of knowledge and creativity, rides on a swan for a vehicle. The swan, which has a sensitive beak that enables it to distinguish pure milk from a mixture of milk and water, symbolizes the ability to discriminate between right and wrong.

Animal guides

The word "animal" is used to represent any living creature: mammals, birds, insects, reptiles, or amphibians. This same process could also be used to connect with plants, minerals, or the elements—earth, air, water, or fire.

Use a blank page in your notebook or journal to glue on pictures of animals that you can find in magazines or on the Internet. Or if you'd like to, you can draw them. Why are you attracted to certain animals and not so much to others? Choose one of your animals and consider the following:

✎ What do you like about this animal?

✎ Have you ever seen this animal in the wild? Where would you go to see it?

✎ Are there qualities in this animal that you can see in yourself?

✎ Are there qualities in this animal that you would like to develop in yourself?

✎ You may want to write a 4-line poem to describe what you know about this animal or how you feel about this animal (the poem doesn't have to rhyme).

✎ You may want to share your thoughts about your animal connection with a close friend!

As you think about
the animals that are important to you,
recognize your connection to all things. Feel one with nature.
Honor your special animals and recognize the special
qualities they model for you. Draw strength from all the
kingdoms and all the beings around you.

*Even after all this
time, the sun
never says to
the Earth,
"you owe me."
Look what
happens with
a love like
that. It lights
the whole sky!*
~Hafiz

Shayna, age 12

Who Is That Girl in the Mirror?

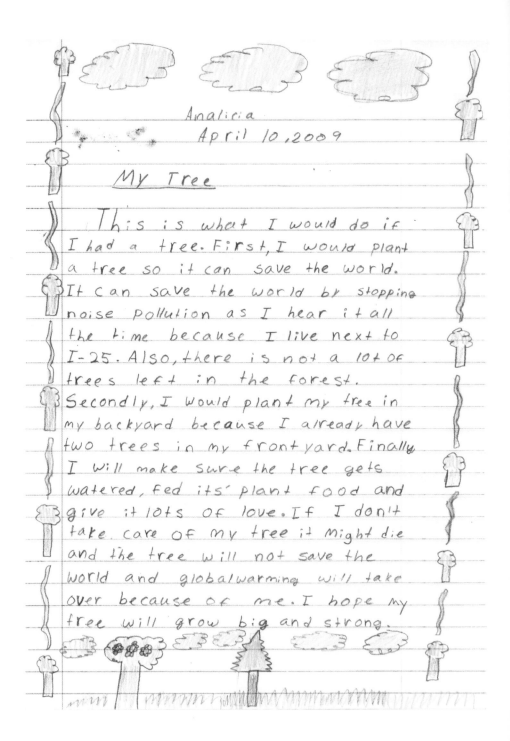

Analicia
April 10, 2009

My Tree

This is what I would do if I had a tree. First, I would plant a tree so it can save the world. It can save the world by stopping noise pollution as I hear it all the time because I live next to I-25. Also, there is not a lot of trees left in the forest. Secondly, I would plant my tree in my backyard because I already have two trees in my front yard. Finally I will make sure the tree gets watered, fed its' plant food and give it lots of love. If I don't take care of my tree it might die and the tree will not save the world and globalwarming will take over because of me. I hope my tree will grow big and strong.

Amaterasu Girl: Tara Church and Tree Musketeers

A strong message of Amaterasu concerns our natural connection with all living things. The plants, the trees, the birds, and the wind are our family, too. As a nine-year-old, Tara Church knew this connection to be true. After a discussion with her Brownie Girl Scout troop about cutting down trees to make paper products, Tara Church had an idea—what if they planted a tree to help the planet? On May 9, 1987, Marcie the Marvelous Tree was planted in El Segundo, California, and as Marcie grew, so did an environmental group called Tree Musketeers. Tara and her friends imagined children all over the world planting trees, and from their vision a movement was started. As the story of their organization spread, they got calls from all over the country from kids wanting to start their own groups. Tree Musketeers was incorporated as a nonprofit corporation that continues to be administered by kids.

Tara and her group believe that neighborhood by neighborhood, kids can save the Earth. One of their roadblocks was a bias against an organization run by kids. Businesses and the media tended to only want to talk to their adult partners. Tree Musketeers decided right then that only kids could speak for their group. They became well prepared and in demand.

Over the next 10 years, they began school programs focusing on the environment and "adopted out thousands of homeless baby trees to loving kids." Tree Musketeers was responsible for planting and maintaining a park-like grove in what was a weed-infested median strip between El Segundo and the Los Angeles airport. But this was just the start. They opened the community's first recycling center and packaged a Hometown Forests program as an action kit that is available to other towns. Leadership, Empowerment, and Action Development (LEAD) is a program where kids in fifth to twelfth grade lead a three-month environmental project. By 2000, the program had reached 1 million kids, hours, and trees!

Although Tara Church has grown up and become a lawyer, she still serves as the chair of the Board of Directors. The organization is more active than ever, and Marcie the Marvelous Tree was declared "famous and historic" and now has her own autobiography. Tree Musketeers started small, but with kid power and dedication, it continues to grow, teach leadership, and fill the planet with the beauty of trees.

For more information about Tree Musketeers and Marcie the Marvelous Tree, go to www.treemusketeers.org.

On Earth Day, April 22, 2009, 29 girls and boys from the Bryant-Webster School in Denver were the first kids in Colorado to register trees with Tree Musketeers for their 3 x 3 project—three million trees planted by three million kids to help offset global warming. To register any trees that you help to plant, visit www.partnersfortheplanet.org.

When we registered our trees, the kids who participated received a certificate from Tree Musketeers. The certificates had this pledge on it:

Earth is our home and she needs our help.
Trees will do their part and I promise to do mine
by being a leader in my community.
I dedicate this tree as part of my effort
to help fight global warming.

Be an Amaterasu Girl!

What will you remember about Amaterasu and her lessons about anger?

What will you remember about Amaterasu and her lessons about letting your light shine?

How did Amaterasu inspire you?

Did you see similarities with yourself and Amaterasu? List your Amaterasu qualities.

How can you be an Amaterasu girl? What can you do? Remember to dream big! Look what Tara Church did.

Remember that making a difference one person at a time is special, too.
Where can you make a difference? Who can you help this week?

Making a difference

How Many Things I Can Be

I am a joke waiting to be told

I am a pen waiting to write great things

I am a book waiting to be read

I am a sapling who is just beginning to take root

I am the sun just beginning to come out after the rain

I am a wanderer dreaming in the moon by night

I am a fairy tale whose magic is yet to be discovered

I am a story yet to read, where people haven't found out
*   the way I am going to be yet.*

I can be all of these things,

And I can still be me.

Kari Olmon, age 13
    (New Moon Magazine,
    May/June 2004)

Inspiration from Amaterasu

I, Amaterasu, see the brilliant
light radiating from you. You are a
kaleidoscope of individuality . . . .
You are discovering how to accept and
work through your anger . . . . You are
connected in a web of life to all beings
and recognize that each living thing
has many lessons for you.

one person at a time

THE SECOND PORTAL OF PRIDE:

Believing in Yourself

CHAPTER

5

Trusting Who You Are

Ophelia opened her eyes as the sun pierced her sleep. She quickly got out of bed as she remembered today was the day she and Mateo were going to visit their father's family ranch, now owned by their Uncle Fredo. Ophelia was eager to see the horses. She was excited because this was the first day she was actually going to ride. She had hung around the horses a few times and had fed them carrots and caressed their soft noses, but they always seemed so big that she had never wanted to actually get on the back of one. She often spent her time at the ranch with her Aunt Marisol, who filled the kitchen with the spicy smell of homemade tamales. Sometimes she took off by herself and hung out at a special place where a creek tumbled over the smooth rocks and the trees shielded her from the hot sun. An occasional crow or magpie would appear wanting a hand-out. One evening, she sat in her special place motionless as a doe and her fawn came to that spot for a drink. She thought of it as her secret hideaway.

Mateo ran to the car ahead of her. He had been riding since he was seven and even at nine had learned how to mount, walk, turn, trot, and gallop. Today Uncle Alfredo, Fredo for short, had promised to show him some roping skills.

Believing in Yourself

Fredo was their father's brother, who had his Mexican mother's dark eyes and hair, and often used Spanish words when speaking to them. He also had a delightful moustache that curved over his lips and down the sides of his mouth. Ophelia felt her uncle favored Mateo because of their common love of horses, and today she was determined to show that she could be a good rider too.

As their father drove in the front gate, two of the ranch dogs came to greet them, wagging their tails and running ahead of the car leading the way into the ranch. Mateo tumbled out of the front seat and ran to the corral. Fredo tousled his hair and said "Bienvenidos!" Mateo noticed that his favorite horse, Shadow, was already saddled, along with another horse, Luz. He immediately climbed on Shadow and began riding around the ring. Her uncle turned to Ophelia and said, "I will help you to ride on Luz today. She is a very calm horse to get you started."

Her father, Rafe, stood outside the corral talking to a woman with red hair that Ophelia knew boarded her horse at the ranch. She was sometimes there when they visited. "Ophelia," Papa said, "come meet Colleen—she rides her horse in many rodeos . . . . I need to help Marisol with some repairs in the kitchen," he continued as he walked toward the house.

Ophelia walked over and shook the hand of the woman whose curly hair was tied back with a bandana. "Hello," she said. "I'm going to learn to ride today."

Colleen smiled and said, "Good luck. I was about your age when I started riding." Ophelia turned back to Uncle Fredo but as she approached Luz, she was shaking with fear. The horse was so big. Why had she agreed to do this? What did she need to prove?

"Okay, Ophelia," Fredo said, as he clasped his hands and leaned over. "Put your left foot on my hands and I'll boost you up." Ophelia lifted her foot and stumbled before she could stand straight with her foot snugly cradled in his hands.

"Hang onto the saddle horn there and as I lift you up, you swing your right leg over the saddle." Ophelia grabbed the saddle horn and just then Luz pulled up her head and snorted, knocking Ophelia off balance and onto the ground.

"You can't be afraid of a little snort. Let's try again." This time Ophelia's legs were trembling as she let go of the saddle horn, just as Fredo pushed her up onto the saddle. Ophelia's legs just wouldn't grip as she tumbled over Luz and landed on the other side, cringing with fear that the horse would step on her.

"Ophelia, you need to relax, chica. This horse won't hurt you. You are too tense and making everyone spooky."

Ophelia felt sick to her stomach. "Could I try again later?" she asked.

"You can't be serious," Fredo moaned. "You're giving up already?" He looked at her with eyes that said he wasn't surprised and turned to talk to Mateo.

Mateo came back around the circle of the corral. "What a wimp," he yelled.

Ophelia's eyes stung with tears as she walked toward the stable for some water. She pulled out her phone from her vest pocket and texted Marissa. "Im such a loser - fell off horse twice."

She immediately received a reply, "get back on."

Colleen, who had watched the scene in the corral, put her arm around her, and said, "Don't take it to heart, Ophelia. No one gets it right the first time. Don't let those guys stop you." She led her to a hay bale where they could sit. Ophelia drank her water so she wouldn't start crying.

"Have you ever heard of Rhiannon?" Colleen asked.

"Yeah," Ophelia answered. "She's in a song that my Mom likes by Fleetwood Mac."

Colleen smiled and said, "Yes she is, but she is also a Celtic goddess who doubts herself when her friends tell lies about her. Would you like to hear the story?"

Ophelia nodded yes, taking a few deep breaths to calm herself. Colleen began the story.

> bienvenidos – welcome
> (bee en ven EE doz)
> chica (CHEE kah) – girl
> Rhiannon (ree AN non)
> Pwyll (poo eel)

"Rhiannon could have had her pick of many gods as a husband, and yet she fell in love with a mortal, Pwyll, the Lord of Dyfed. Even though he didn't know she existed, she would often watch him when he was out riding. She loved the way his golden hair moved in the wind, brushing back across his face. His steel blue eyes brightened with the joy of the ride.

"Finally, one day Rhiannon decided to approach Pwyll, and she could have just shown herself to him, but Rhiannon never did anything in a simple, ordinary way . . . .

"Pwyll rode toward a hill behind the royal court even though he had been warned to stay away from that place. He was told that when a man of royal blood would sit on that hill, one of two things would happen: the royal man received a terrible beating or he saw something wonderful. The men encouraged him not to risk it, but Pwyll was willing to take a chance. As he sat there with his men, he saw Rhiannon ride by on her white horse. Quite entranced with her, he sent one of his horsemen after her, but she rode so fast, she disappeared before the man could reach her. Hoping to see this woman again, Pwyll and his men went to the hill the following day. When Rhiannon appeared, Pwyll sent a man on the fastest horse after her; still, she could not be caught. On the third day, Pwyll, who by this time was completely entranced by this beautiful woman, rode after her himself."

"Do you think I will ever be able to ride so fast?" Ophelia interrupted with a moan.

"You can't ride fast unless you start slowly," Colleen answered and gave her a hug as she continued with the story.

"When Pwyll's horse finally tired of the chase, he yelled at Rhiannon to please stop and talk to him. She paused, turned, and waited for him. 'Where are you going?' Pwyll asked.

"I have come to see you," Rhiannon answered with a wry smile.

"Well, you're going in the wrong direction!' Pwyll answered. To his surprise, Rhiannon told him that her father was giving her to a man in marriage against her will. Without wasting words, she told him that she did not want to marry the man because she had been watching Pwyll and had fallen in love with him. She spoke so eloquently about her belief in the power of love, asking if he, instead, would take her hand in marriage."

"Oh, my, I cannot be-*lieve* it," reacted Ophelia, "She just met the guy!"

"I know," assured Coleen, "This probably would never happen today, but that was another time . . . and after all, we are talking about a goddess in a desperate situation. She was about to be married off!"

Colleen continued with the story, "By now, Pwyll was so smitten by this straightforward young woman who could ride like the wind, that he answered, 'If I had my choice of every girl and woman in the world, I would choose you.' Rhiannon and Pwyll were married exactly a year later in her father's court."

"Well, at least they had a year-long engagement!" Ophelia was feeling a bit better about this strange story. Dating and boys were still topics she was unsure about, and at the same time, she had begun to be a little opinionated about a few things. After all, you had to be—between the well-meaning talks of parents, the sex ed and self-esteem workshops in school, what your girlfriends said, and then, of course, the boys. Yikes! It was a pool of things to think about, and all a girl could do was to try to find out what she believed was right for her; to find her own way in a sea of expectations and demands . . . . Ophelia listened intently as the story continued.

"The newlyweds ruled the kingdom in prosperity and love. Their love spread throughout their kingdom, bringing joy and happiness to the entire land. In the third year, Rhiannon bore a son. They were so happy! There was a huge celebration in the court. Six of her handmaidens spent the first night with her to take care of her and the beloved child. It was their job to watch over the child in the night, but all of the women fell asleep and when they awoke the baby was gone! How could this happen? To save themselves, they quickly thought of a plan to hide their awful mistake. Instead of telling the royal mother what had happened, they killed some deerhound pups, smeared the blood on Rhiannon's face and laid the bones near her body."

"I don't like that they killed puppies," Ophelia sighed. "What a terrible, disgusting thing to do to Rhiannon. And by the way, how could the baby have disappeared to begin with?"

Nicola, age 12

Believing in Yourself

"You'll find out, Ophelia. What happens next is an important part of the story," Colleen replied. "Should I continue?" Yes, nodded Ophelia, her eyes wide with curiosity.

"When Rhiannon awoke, she dreamily asked for the child. She was told in shock and horror by the women that she had killed and eaten her baby in the night. She could not believe she could do such a thing to her dear child, but the evidence made her doubt herself. The blood and bones were there on her mouth and her hands. Even for a self-assured goddess like Rhiannon, there was reason to doubt. The voice inside her said 'no,' she could not have done this unthinkable act, because she loved her baby so much, yet her handmaidens convinced her otherwise in order to save their own skins.

Alexandra,
age 14

"Because of his great love for her, Pwyll would not send her away as many people suggested, but he did agree to give her a punishment. For seven years, Rhiannon was sentenced to remain near the gate of the court of Dyfed and tell her shocking story to all strangers who came to visit the palace. She then had to offer to carry guests to the court on her back. She had to carry her humiliation both emotionally and physically, so that she would never again know peace. Her despair was so profound, for she no longer believed in herself or in the power of her love.

"Meanwhile, Teirnon, the lord of a nearby land who possessed a well-known and beautiful mare, waited for her to foal on the first day of May, as she did every year. In the dark of the night, for some unknown reason, the foal always disappeared. On May 1st, Teirnon decided to bring the mare inside and keep watch that night. The foal was born easily, but at the moment of birth, there was a loud noise and a great claw came through the window to seize the foal. Teirnon drew his sword and hacked off the arm at the elbow. Hearing a scream, he opened the door, but he saw nothing in the darkness. Looking down, he found a small child, wrapped in a silk blanket lying beside the door."

"Wow," Ophelia said, leaning closer to Colleen, "I have a feeling this baby is the one that Rhiannon lost—am I right?"

Colleen smiled but didn't say a word in response to Ophelia's question. "Teirnon gave the baby to his wife," she continued, "who was thrilled to raise him for they had no children. The child had golden yellow hair and was always stronger than any of the boys his age. They loved him as if he was their own son.

"Eventually Teirnon heard about the unexplained disappearance of the Rhiannon and Pwyll's child, and how Rhiannon was being punished for harming her son. He realized that his son closely resembled Pwyll. Although Teirnon did not want to give up his dear sweet child, he knew in his heart that this boy was their missing son. He understood the anguish that the birth parents must be feeling, so he took the child to the court and presented him to Rhiannon and Pwyll.

"Immediately upon seeing the child, they recognized him as their own. Pwyll and Rhiannon were overcome with joy and wonder to see their son alive. He had been treated with love and care, so Teirnon and his wife were given a great reward, and it was agreed that they would continue to see the young boy.

"Rhiannon was absolved of her crime and given her rightful place alongside Pwyll. Again they ruled over the land in love and peace. Rhiannon learned to know and trust the voice inside of her—the one which told her that she could not possibly have done such a horrible thing as to kill and eat her child. From that day forward, no matter what happened, Rhiannon never doubted her inner truth again.

Ophelia had listened so carefully to the story that she forgot her embarrassment and fear. She wondered why she believed it when people told her she couldn't do things. She had been eager to try this morning, and had given into embarrassment when she felt like such a klutz. But her fear that she just couldn't do it got worse when she was criticized by Uncle Fredo and Mateo.

Girls say it best!

"Never let fear get in the way of your ambitions."

Shayna age 14

"Colleen," she said, "could you help me get on Luz and take me around the corral?"

"Of course, Ophelia," Colleen stood up and held out her hand. "I will show you some ways to make it easier." Colleen let Ophelia stand on a wooden box that she pulled out of the barn. It made Ophelia feel taller than the horse and it was so much easier to swing her leg over as Colleen held her body steady.

"Just sit for a few minutes and feel the horse beneath your legs. Feel her breathe. Watch her ears turn toward you as you say her name softly to her and tell her how beautiful she is. Remember that Luz means 'light' in Spanish."

Ophelia leaned forward and whispered, "Luz, you are a beam of light from the sun—you are so beautiful. I will ride you today around the corral and we will get to know each other. I will learn what I need to know to communicate with you."

After several circuits of the corral, Ophelia dismounted with Colleen's help and hugged her with a sense of relief that she had survived and had actually enjoyed it! Then she gave Luz a carrot and smiled with a smile that lit up her whole face. "And someday, Luz," she said, "we will ride like the wind."

Things to remind you of Rhiannon:

Irish or Welsh scarf with pictures of Celtic knot symbols

Pictures of Celtic knot symbols from the Internet

Statues or pictures of birds

Statues or pictures of horses

Rhiannon picture from Internet

Rhiannon card from goddess card deck

Go to www.opheliasoracle.com to see our favorites!

You have passed through

Ophelia's first Portal of Pride. "Who is

that girl in the mirror?" is not only the place to

begin, but is a place that you will return to again and

again. Knowing who you are is a lifetime process! It is a pre-

cious gift to develop the skills necessary to truly see yourself.

Then, you can choose to live your life as only you can. Instead of

trying to copy someone else's way of being—you can do it your way!

Develop a healthy sense of appreciation for the unique person who

you are. There are so many special things about you! Take out your

doubts, examine them, and learn from them. Realize just how much

you have to offer . . . . Cross the next threshold into the second

Portal of Pride, as you move into an important discovery:

Believing in Yourself

6
Managing Self-Doubt

How often do we take
critical and negative comments
said by someone else
and start believing them about ourselves?

Rhiannon actually believed that she had killed and eaten her baby in the night because of the assurances of trusted friends and what looked like evidence to support their story. She gave in to believing the fabricated lies of others, rather than believing in her own inner truth.

> Bullying for girls, especially tweens and early teens,
> includes telling lies, sending angry e-mails or texts,
> exclusion from the group, and sharing closely-held secrets.
> Girls fight with relationships instead of fists.
>
> Excerpt from Rachel Simmons
> *Odd Girl Out: The Hidden Culture of Aggression in Girls*

Discouraging words

Sometimes other people say discouraging words to us. And sometimes, we say discouraging words to ourselves. When we listen to discouraging words, we begin to have doubts about ourselves. Rhiannon listened to her friends who lied about how her baby disappeared. She lost her sense of self.

> Do you believe it when someone else says something negative about you?

> Do you believe it when you say something negative about someone else?

> What would your life be like if you never doubted yourself because of what someone else said about you?

Imagine someone saying, "You look really weird because you have a pointed head."

– What would your response be?

– Does that statement make you feel bad? Probably not!

– Why not? Because most likely you don't have a pointed head, so why would the comment make you feel bad?

Now imagine someone saying to you, "You are a mean, selfish person."

– Would that statement make you feel bad? Many girls would say yes.

– And why do you think that is?

It should only make you feel bad if you believe it to be true. If you believe you are not a mean, selfish person, then that statement can't hurt you any more than the statement about your pointed head.

Often it is our doubt about ourselves that gets triggered by others' words. Those sensitive, tender places need compassion and understanding, so they may heal and no longer be places of insecurity.

"No matter what you say or do to me,
I still know I'm a worthwhile person."

Rea, age 12

Tanya and Karen have been friends for several years. They are discussing Todd, a boy in their class who is popular and good looking. Tanya mentions for the fourth time that she really likes Todd and wonders how to get him to notice her. After being silent for awhile, Karen admits she has a secret crush on Todd too. Tanya, with an ugly look at Karen, walks away and begins to spread lies about Karen and calls her a bitch. Karen wonders what she did wrong and why her friend would turn on her so quickly.

 Why do you think Tanya got angry and turned on Karen?

 Should Karen have continued to keep her secret feelings for Todd a secret from her good friend Tanya?

 Is it typical for girls to lash out at each other because they like the same boy? If so, why do you think that happens?

 Why do girls sometimes deliberately try to ruin another girl's reputation?

A letting go activity

On a piece of paper or in your journal, write down three of the most negative things you have ever said to yourself—or that someone else has said to you.

Take this paper and tear it into the smallest bits you can and throw it away.

Say, "I release these negative words and thoughts. They no longer affect me."

Believing in Yourself

Note to self: Don't worry what other people think of my self and try not to listen to what other people say. Make new friends, tell people the truth, and try not to care so much what people do and say. Don't let people get to me. I need to think about the real truth and don't listen to the things that aren't true.

Samatha, age 8

Mind Chatter

Sometimes our minds just keep chattering away about how stupid we are—or how ugly or uncoordinated. We also believe it if others tease us. Tina had a big brother who often called her a dope. She had to tune him out and remind herself that she was not a dope, that she was smart and got good grades and had friends. Donna moved to a new town and switched schools when she was in seventh grade, and for a whole year, all of the "in" girls made fun of her. There was one girl who even wanted to beat her up!

Have you ever experienced being on the outside looking in?

 What if people you think are your friends turn on you and start teasing or criticizing? What can you do?

 Do you sometimes make it worse by believing the terrible things somebody else says about you?

Girls Who Rule the School

One girl shared that she was afraid
of the "girls who rule the school."
Who are they? ". . . the girls who wear clothes that the boys like."
Guess how old she is? Eight!

Balancing the negative with the positive

Jade, age 8

Write something true about yourself.
What is something you are really proud of?

Believing in Yourself

✎ On a piece of paper or in your journal, write several positive things about yourself.

✎ See the list on the next page for ideas for positive words that will help you describe yourself.

✎ Look at your list whenever someone tries to make you feel bad about yourself.

– Are you mirthful or hilarious or joyful?

– Are you calm and serene and tender?

– If you're not sure what some of the words mean, take some time to look them up.

– If you say these words to describe yourself or make positive statements about yourself every day for the next three weeks, your brain will start believing it.

Just think what you could say inside yourself the next time a negative thought comes up:

"I hear you suggesting that I am a klutz . . . and I'm not believing that to be true about me just because I tripped. I know I am outrageously excellent at basketball, and that takes coordination!"

Or, "I refuse to believe that I am a loser, because I am blissfully soaring about my good grades in English class!"

Try it!

What comes first: a smile or the good feeling?
Research has shown that having a positive attitude by making positive statements and smiling increases one's sense of well-being and happiness.

Encouraging words

adorable	delighted		
playful	outrageously		
hilarious	easily		
clever	liberated		
bright	optimistic		
joyful	ecstatic		
beautiful	overjoyed		
joyous	peaceful		
blissful	pleasant		
jubilant	enchanted		
free	pleased		
zany	enjoying		
calm	purring	fulfilled	tender
juicy	enthusiastic	fun-loving	grateful
celebrating	quiet	satisfied	thrilled
lively	excellent	gentle	tranquil
affectionate	spirited	serene	happy
lucky	terrific	glad	having fun
centered	excited	soaring	wonderful
cheerful	warmhearted	gorgeous	courageous
loving	exhilarated	sweetly	fantastic
confident	rejoicing	graceful	generous
content	energized	stunning	certain
mirthful	relaxed	great	successful

Believing your own sense of "knowing"

Rhiannon didn't listen to the voice inside of her—the one that told her that she could not possibly have done such a horrible thing as to kill and eat her child. Think about the punishment Rhiannon endured because she believed the lies that were told about her. Too bad they didn't have bone specialists back then who could tell her immediately that the blood and bones she woke up with were canine and not human! She needed Crime Scene Investigation (CSI) for sure . . . .

It's So Easy

It's so easy to forget
when the world takes notice
and our longings all cascade
because we are free
It's so easy to get lost
in requests and warnings
as the chorus asserts itself
about what to be

But I know the reason
There is another step to take
I know the way
I've had it all along, and it's so easy
if I can
just stay planted—here I am
I remember, yeah

Cara Cantarella
from the CD, Now I Know
www.caracantarella.com

Every one of us has an "inner voice" or "gut feeling," which we call intuition. Our intuition picks up clues from the environment, other people, and our own previous experiences, rolls these clues all together, and gives us a message about what is the truth for us. It also reaches out into that undefined larger picture and sometimes alerts us to pieces we do not consciously know.

As we grow up, we are taught over and over to analyze a situation with our brains, our intellect. We forget to listen to our inner knowing. After a while the inner feelings become so faint, we don't even know they are there; so, we often can't access them anymore.

When you hear a statement about someone, do you immediately know whether or not it is true? You can practice listening to your intuition.

✴ Quiet down, take a deep breath, and listen to the voice inside. Don't analyze. Just listen.

✴ Is the inner voice telling you YES, or NO?

✴ More often than not, your first answer will be right. This is true especially if you teach yourself to listen and to trust the answer.

Believing in Yourself

What if a friend asks you to go to a party that will be so much fun because there won't be any adults there? Can you let your intuition guide you about your answer to this invitation? What if your inner voice says NO, but you decide to go anyway because you don't want to seem like a weirdo, or you don't want to hurt your friend's feelings? Okay, suppose your parents find out and ground you for three weeks. Would you begin to trust your intuition then?

 What if Rhiannon had believed in her love for her child enough to "know" that she could not possibly have committed such a terrible act against him?

 What if she strongly stood up for herself and said, "No, something else happened here, and we're going to find out what it was. I am not guilty. It is not possible." Do you think someone would have figured out the truth?

You have an inner knowing about what is right for you, about what is the truth, about who is really your friend.

Just remember, no one knows you like you do.

Listen to that intuition. As you practice trusting this inner knowing, occasionally you may not listen completely, or you may confuse your knowing with your thinking, but don't give up. The more you choose to listen to your intuition, the stronger it will be.

Helping others helps you feel good

Colleen is very kind to Ophelia when she notices the girl's apprehension about riding. How did that kindness affect Ophelia?

What could you do to make one of your classmates, friends, or family members know how much you appreciate him or her? When you take the first step to reach out to someone, often they follow your lead.

Here is the start of the list. Add your own ideas. (Hint: Think of ways you like to be treated.)

* Pay a compliment to a friend
* Do an unexpected chore at home
* Eat lunch with someone new
* Make something for a friend
* Plan a fun surprise for someone

Every day this week, do one of the things on your list. It not only makes other people feel appreciated but it will make you feel good too!

Girls say it Best!

"I learned that the horses act like you act."
Is that true for people, too?

Diana, age 12

Strong Roots

Before there were books, stories were told over and over again, and many of the stories changed over time as the people who told them and the cultures that they belonged to changed. The myth of Rhiannon originally came from the Celtic peoples of Britain. The Celts were tribes from Central Europe who settled in the British Isles 2,500 years ago. Because the Celts did not have a written language, much of what we know about them stems from archeological evidence and from writings by the Romans who conquered much of the Celtic lands.

Let's look at what we know about the status of women in Celtic society. Rulers were usually men, but there were also some famous women rulers, too. Roman authors report that a Celtic woman could not be married without her own consent and had the right to choose her husband, a right that Roman women did not have. In Celtic marriage, men and women were treated equally, because marriage was based on a contract protected by law and was not a religious union. The woman brought her own personal property, given to her by her family, into the marriage and could leave with it in case of divorce, plus she could take a portion of what was acquired during the marriage. Wow! The Celts had a high respect for women.

To the Celts, Rhiannon was an important goddess. She was often accompanied by three birds who had the power to put the living to sleep for years and to awaken the dead. It was no wonder that Pwyll's men warned him not to sit on that particular hill where Rhiannon could be seen by mortals! Rhiannon was also a shapeshifter and often appeared as a white horse. There are many variations of the Rhiannon story; Ophelia heard one version shared by the gentle horsewoman, Colleen. If you find that you are interested in learning more, perhaps you could research the Celts and Rhiannon on your own. Some girls have even told us that they studied the Celts and heard Rhiannon's story as a part of their geography class in school.

Girls supporting each other

After Ophelia's first ride with Luz, Colleen asked if she wanted to ride regularly. "I am here several times a week," Colleen told Ophelia, "and I could spend some time with you if you wish. When I was 12, my family didn't have horses, but I volunteered at a stable nearby where the wranglers took tourists for rides into Rocky Mountain National Park. No matter what they asked me to do, I did it. I spent a lot of time mucking out the stalls."

"What is that?" Ophelia asked.

"Shoveling all the horse poop out from the stalls into a big pile outside." Colleen smiled as she said it.

"That doesn't sound fun at all!" Ophelia exclaimed.

"For me, it was about being with the horses. Nothing was more important than that. I didn't have money for riding lessons, and I just wanted to get to know the horses and learn everything about them. Finally one of the women wranglers volunteered to show me how to ride on her free time.

"I loved the feeling riding gave me. It totally changed my life. I was there every day all summer for six years. Then I was ready for the rodeo circuit.

"Ophelia, I would like to pass on what my friend taught me about connecting with horses. Horses and humans have a deep intuitive sense about each other. I can tell that you will begin to feel that intuitive sense as you get to know Luz. So, what do you think?"

Colleen looked out at the horses as she waited for Ophelia's answer. She didn't have to wait long.

"Yes, yes, yes," Ophelia answered. "And I will sing songs to Luz, and you can tell me stories, and I will learn how to muck out the stalls," she said all in one breath. "When I whispered to Luz, I did feel like she understood me. I love Luz . . . when can we start?"

Do girls help each other?

Colleen reached out to Ophelia. She wanted to pass along what had been taught to her.

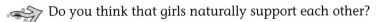 Do you think that girls naturally support each other?

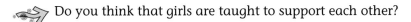 Do you think that girls are taught to support each other?

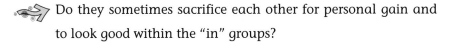 Do they sometimes sacrifice each other for personal gain and to look good within the "in" groups?

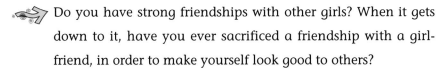 Do you have strong friendships with other girls? When it gets down to it, have you ever sacrificed a friendship with a girlfriend, in order to make yourself look good to others?

> ## • Think About It •
>
> In your experience, how do girls help each other?

Believing in Yourself

Protecting yourself

Rhiannon's story is extreme, and yet we all need to discover and develop ways to physically, mentally, and emotionally protect ourselves.

* We wear the proper clothing to protect ourselves physically. You would not wear shorts in extremely cold weather, although some of you may do that in the winter sometimes!

* Safety-conscious bike riders wear helmets to protect their heads and often padded shorts to protect their bottoms!

* Taking care of our bodies is a personal responsibility; it is originally your parent's job, but as you grow older, more and more of it falls to you. If you take care of your body now, it will serve you for many years to come . . . for after all, it is the little "mobile home" that carries your personality, the unique you, wherever you need to go in the world. Without it, where would you be?

There are times when you need protection against people who are mean, cruel, or want to cause you harm.

* Have you had a friend who gossiped behind your back?

* Do you know a bully at school who picks on you and others?

Using your imagination to create a light-shield

Do you know that you can create your own invisible body shield of protection in your imagination which will defend you against the meanness of people?

Close your eyes and sit quietly. Imagine your shield. There are absolutely no rules about how it should look or feel. Is it metal like a Celtic breastplate? Or is it a soft cloak that covers you from head to toe? It could be as tough as leather or as light as feathers. It could even be tattoos, which are used by the Maori, the indigenous people of New Zealand, for prayers of protection. Think about what it is made of, its weight and color. Does it have special designs, and what do they look like? How will you keep it on? As you create this shield in your mind, imagine that it will keep you safe, because it will remind you of your own inner strength.

No one needs to even know that you are doing it. It is an inside job!

✎ You may want to draw a picture of your light-shield on a piece of paper or in your journal. Use colored pencils and stickers if you wish.

Nicola, age 14

Now take time to try on your light-shield in your mind: strap the straps or tie the ribbons, or step into it. How do you feel with your shield in place? Say these words or make up your own:

I pull forward all of my inner strength.

In times of challenge, I trust what I know to be true.

I express myself with confidence and certainty.

I draw in support both from outside resources and from inner guidance.

I am strong. I am safe.

After you have created a vision of your light-shield, you can use it anytime you want. Imagine it quickly when someone is doing or saying something hurtful, by putting the tips of your thumb and first finger together, and say to yourself, "I believe in myself. I know I am protected by my light-shield."

CHAPTER 8

Being Brave

"Courage is being scared to death but saddling up anyway."

John Wayne

John Wayne is a famous actor who played western heroes
known for riding in and saving the day!

If I Were Brave
What would I do if I knew that I could not fail
If I believed would the wind always fill up my sail
How far would I go, what could I achieve
Trusting the hero in me

Chorus: If I were brave I'd walk the razor's edge
Where fools and dreamers dare to tread
And never lose faith, even when losing my way
What step would I take today if I were brave
What would I do today if I were brave (4x)

What if we're all meant to do what we secretly dream
What would you ask if you knew you could have anything
Like the mighty oak sleeps in the heart of a seed
Are there miracles in you and me

Chorus

If I refuse to listen to the voice of fear
Would the voice of courage whisper in my ear

Chorus

To listen to
or download
this song, go to
itunes.com

If I Were Brave, Jana Stanfield/Jimmy Scott
Jana StanTunes/English Channel Music (ASCAP)
www.JanaStanfield.com

Girls say it Best!

"I learned how not to stay on the horse!"

Although Ophelia's Dad, Rafe, didn't have time to ride horses much anymore, he happily agreed to go with Ophelia when she asked him to join her at Uncle Alfredo's ranch. She had been learning how to ride from Colleen for several weeks and wanted her father to see how much she had improved. She made a picnic lunch of sandwiches, apples, and cookies and put them in her daypack along with two water bottles. Rafe smiled as Ophelia chattered about her life on the drive; they didn't often get to have time alone, and he was grateful that she was in such a good mood.

Shadow and Luz were saddled when they arrived, so Rafe put the food in his saddlebag and waited to see if Ophelia needed help getting on Luz. She spoke gently to the horse first, telling her exactly what she was going to do, then put her foot in the stirrup, grabbed the saddlehorn and swung up onto the saddle. She held the reins in her left hand and looked over at her Dad, who was just beginning to mount Shadow. "Hurry up, slowpoke," Ophelia said, teasing him with a smile.

They headed for the area of the ranch the family called the Redlands, because the red rocks rising from the grassland looked like they had been pushed from the earth in a moment of anger and then toppled on their sides as the earth shook in disgust. They had their own stark beauty, and the millions of years of exposure to rain and wind had softened and rounded them, leaving high walls in some places and wide openings in others. There were many cattle trails they could follow, and Rafe knew every one of them from his early rides with his older brother Alfredo when they were growing up.

Ophelia had never ridden into the Redlands but had skirted the bottom a few times before she headed back with Colleen by her side. She was learning to canter and loved feeling the movement of the horse beneath her. Her fear had subsided, and she looked forward to learning how to respond to the different rhythms as Luz trotted, moved and turned, slowed and walked.

Rafe took Ophelia up a trail that led to the ridge of the Redlands. Both horses had walked this trail many times and seemed to feel steady in the familiar surroundings. When they reached a place where the trail leveled off, Rafe stopped the horses and suggested it was a good place for lunch. They dismounted, tied up the horses in a shady spot, grabbed the lunches, and scrambled up some rocks to get to the highest point. Ophelia almost stumbled when she looked out over the red rock canyons to the grassland below . . . she was feeling dizzy from the height and leaned back as her father steadied her with his arm around her shoulder. Slowly, she relaxed, sat down to each lunch, and quietly admired the view.

"Dad, this is the most beautiful place I have ever been. Why didn't you talk about it or bring me here before?" Ophelia asked.

"Because it is a sacred place, Ophelia.
We believe you can come here when you are ready to listen
to the pulse of nature and feel the energies of the Earth."

"What does that mean, Dad?" Ophelia looked at her father in wonder.

"It means you are old enough to understand that early peoples considered this to be sacred land, where they held ceremonies to honor important events in their lives: the naming of a child, a marriage, a death. They believed that all life has a rhythm that occurs in different lengths of time. Do you remember when you were studying about the gestation periods of dogs, elephants, and other animals?"

Believing in Yourself

"Sure, elephants carry their babies for two years before they are born, but puppies are born in two months," Ophelia commented brightly.

"Trees have an even slower rhythm, don't they? They live much longer than humans, some for hundreds of years. But what about rocks? Their rhythm of being born from the earth and being worn away by rain, wind, or floods can take thousands or even millions of years. Yet they change like we do. Follow me, I want to show you something." Ophelia's dad walked with her about 20 feet to a large flat rock, warmed by the sun, where they lay down on their backs. "This was once an inland sea, Ophelia, and occasionally I have found fossil shells here. Take some deep breaths and listen quietly to the natural sounds. When you are ready, tell me what you hear."

Ophelia breathed, closed her eyes, and listened intently. "I hear the rustling of the leaves of the scrub oak in the breeze, a couple of chickadees calling to each other, and the horses snorting to each other. But there is something deeper, so deep I'm not sure whether I heard it or felt it. Like a heartbeat. Is it yours?"

Rafe smiled. "Dear daughter,
you are feeling the vibrations from the Earth.

There are many things moving far, far below us, such as water, oil, and gas. Sometimes if you put your ear to the Earth, you can hear the vibrations of animals, people or rivers on the surface of the Earth. We are linked in ways that you can't imagine unless you take time to listen."

"Oh Dad, will you bring me out here again sometime?" Ophelia asked enthusiastically. "I want to see what else I can hear and feel."

Just then, they heard a loud whinny from Shadow, and both horses seemed to be bumping into each other. Rafe jumped up and ran down the rocks to see what was disturbing them. A rattlesnake had emerged from a crevice in the rocks near the horses, and they were highly agitated by its warning rattle. Rafe grabbed Luz's reins and led her away from the snake. Ophelia petted Luz and talked to her softly. When Rafe turned to get Shadow, the horse reared up in fear, knocking him backwards. He felt his foot catch between two rocks and heard a loud snap as he fell.

By this time, the snake had escaped to safety and Shadow was visibly calmer. Rafe, however, could feel searing pain travel up his leg from his ankle. Ophelia tied Luz and ran to her father. "Dad, are you all right?"

"No, I think I broke my ankle in that fall," he said with a grimace. It was already swelling, and the pain was intense.

"Ophelia, you must take Luz and go get Fredo. Tell him to bring something to stabilize this leg. I won't be able to ride down otherwise."

"I don't want to leave you alone," Ophelia said, her eyes growing wide. She had never ridden anywhere by herself.

"You must. I know you can do it," Rafe said, forcing a smile. "Luz knows the way back to the barn. You won't get lost, but be careful—I don't want you getting hurt, too."

Ophelia mounted Luz and remembered to talk to her calmly before they started off. They walked down the trail to where the rocks met the grass. Ophelia could see where she and her Dad had entered the red rock trail. She could also see the ranch house and barn far off in the distance.

Believing in Yourself

She thought for a moment of Rhiannon and tightened up the reins. She leaned forward and whispered to Luz, "Ride like the wind, my beautiful lady; I'll try to stay on." She kicked her sides, and Luz took off at a gallop. Ophelia knew she would fall off if she kept her legs and arms so stiff . . . she loosened her limbs and let her body flow with the rhythm of the horse.

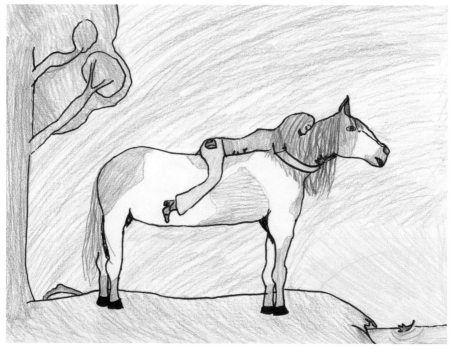

Kayla, age 11

Never had she ridden so fast or felt so urgent. Luz slowed down when she approached the barn, and Ophelia saw that Uncle Fredo had been watching them run.

"Dad's hurt up on the Redlands Ridge," she said breathlessly. "He needs you to bring something to stabilize his leg so he can ride down. A rattlesnake spooked Shadow, and Dad's foot got caught in a hole. He thinks his ankle is broken."

"I'll get Hank to help," Pito said. "He's here today moving some cows around. You stay here with your aunt —I'm sure she's got lemonade inside. Walk Luz twice around the corral to cool her down first." He headed off to get some splints and saddle his horse, when he turned and looked at her intently and with some pride in his voice said, "That was some fast riding, chica."

Getting back on the horse

Have you ever tried to do something without getting it right the very first time? Of course you have! It happens to all of us, because life is an opportunity to grow through our experiences. If we never tried new things or learned new skills, we would never even get out of diapers!

Ophelia would have missed the excitement of the wind in her hair in a full gallop, if she had not had the courage and the tenacity to keep getting back on that horse while she cultivated the skills necessary to be a good rider.

 What skills have you taken the time to develop?

 What have you "failed" at initially and then revisited later?

 Is it really a bad thing to try something and to have it turn out differently than you would like? Do you ever learn from the experience and then try again?

From the horse's mouth:

I took the air deep in my lungs today . . . .

taking in the scent of the air. Hope filled my nostrils and the scent of all possibility that lays ahead for you, smelled sweet and fresh.

Enjoy the trail.

Wisdom, age unknown

An actual spokeshorse from Touched by a Horse Melisa Pearce www.touchedbyahorse.com

Believing in Yourself

✎ Look at this fun letter puzzle that Donna created for the word FAILING. She came up with a meaningful word for each letter creating a phrase that she believes accurately describes what that word (failing) means.

F	Fabulous	**S**	_____
A	Attempt	**U**	_____
I	In	**C**	_____
L	Leaping	**C**	_____
I	Into	**E**	_____
N	New	**S**	_____
G	Growth	**S**	_____

Can you create another possibility for the word FAILURE and one for the word SUCCESS? We'd love to see what you come up with . . . . Send us your ideas at www.opheliasoracle.com.

Fabulous attempt in leaping into new growth . . . Mylie Cyrus and her father, Billie Rae Cyrus, talked about this very thing on The Oprah Show. They said that the great inventor Thomas Edison was a role model for their family. Edison believed that every failure brought you closer to success, because every failure was an opportunity to learn from what does not work, so you could formulate what does. The old adage, "if at first you don't succeed, try, try again" goes a long way to encouraging us to keep on trying. The true value is not only in the destination one arrives at when she experiences the point of success, but in the action of each and every step along the path.

During one of our "Fabulously Fun Focus Fests," three girls came up with this "Success" idea:

S Support

U Us

C Children

C Creating

E Excitement

S So

S Sincerely

Thanks to Rylie 12, Jade 8, and Aspen 7 !

Thomas Edison said,
"If we did all the things we are capable of,
we would literally astound ourselves."

CHAPTER 9

Rhiannon Girl: Melanie Torres and Medicine Horse Program

Rhiannon, the horse goddess, learned the hard way how to believe in herself, rather than listen to what other people said about her. The first time Melanie Torres rode a horse at age 12, she was uncertain, apprehensive, and downright terrified before the experience. She and many other girls in the Latina Leadership Group at her middle school were worried about what might happen once they got on the horses at the stable. They had seen too many TV shows and movies of horses rearing up and riders falling off. The 90-minute trail ride increased Melanie's comfort level, but she didn't have to do much but sit and follow the horse in front of her. Although the stable ride was fun, the girls didn't really connect with the horses they rode.

During Melanie's seventh grade year, she and the Leadership Group got to visit the Medicine Horse Program each month to learn more about horses. The Program is designed to teach life skills to youth, adults, families, and groups through therapeutic interaction with horses.

The first day they arrived, the girls were in a corral with the horses and told that they could choose a horse—but most likely a horse would choose them. Melanie tried to pet a couple of horses, but it was Patrick, a former racehorse, who immediately followed her around. After that, Melanie chose Patrick to work with on every visit because of the special bond she felt with him.

For six months, the girls groomed the horses, walked them around the corral, and even did an obstacle course holding onto their horses' harnesses—before they were allowed to ride. To Melanie, this time was important, and Medicine Horse day was her favorite day of the month. She said, "Patrick could sense my moods, and just knowing I was going to be with him put me in a happy, confident mood."

Melanie feels that being with horses taught her that "you can express yourself in any way and that you shouldn't be afraid." She learned to be herself and know that others would listen. Despite her fears about being with horses at first, Melanie learned the importance of trying new things. "Otherwise," she said, "I would always just have to wonder what it would be like."

Melanie Torres—Rhiannon girl—has learned to trust herself and her love of animals so much that she signed up to volunteer at the local Humane Society and work there weekly. And she has an even bigger goal in mind . . . to someday be a veterinarian!

You can learn about the very special riding programs at Medicine Horse by visiting www.medicinehorse.org. Also, you can go to the www.ohorse.com/stables/therapeutic-riding website to find therapeutic riding stables all over the U.S. and the world.

Be a Rhiannon Girl!

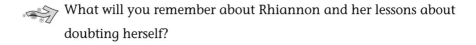

What will you remember about Rhiannon and her lessons about doubting herself?

Did you see similarities with yourself and Rhiannon?
List your Rhiannon qualities.

How can you be a Rhiannon girl? How did Melanie Torres inspire you to try something new?

Do you remember our suggestions of how to get rid of negative thoughts? And how could you replace the negative with positive thoughts?

Are you ready to let your intuition guide you?

What is your favorite part of this Portal of Pride: Believing in Yourself?

Inspiration from Rhiannon

I, Rhiannon, admire your confident self. You are learning to listen to that inner voice which will help guide you in times of doubt. You are moving forward in the world knowing how to turn negative thoughts into positive ones. Nothing can stop you from reaching your dreams.

Listen to your inner voice

THE THIRD PORTAL OF PRIDE:

The Power of One

CHAPTER 10

Compassion

Ophelia savored every moment of Obachan's visit. She adored her grandmother, and the feeling was absolutely mutual. There was a common place where they connected, which was totally unique to the two of them.

"Two peas in a pod," Ophelia liked to say.

The relationship was magical, really and yet, it was very practical, too. Ophelia felt as if she could understand the secrets of the universe, while curled in the safety of her grandmother's lap. And Chiyo's confidence, and steady approach to life, rubbed off on the young girl. With Chiyo, all things seemed possible.

But now the time was approaching for Chiyo to return to Japan. She had stayed for over a month now, and her six-week trip was coming to a close. The two had enjoyed many adventures together, and for Ophelia, anything she did with Obachan was the very best.

The days were getting longer and warmer, and on this particular day, the family was headed for Mateo's school picnic. Ophelia loved the park they were going to, and she was happy just to be hanging out with the whole family. There was an open meadow, where the games were held, and there were picnic tables around the perimeter, shaded by cottonwood trees.

The Power of One

The picnic was okay as picnics went, and the day was beautiful, so Ophelia was having a fun time. She had just settled down with her constant companion, the "emergency book" she carried with her just in case she got bored. Ophelia could always get lost in a good story! Her concentration was distracted by some shouting close by; she observed that a group of older boys were taunting Ryan, a boy from Mateo's class. Ryan had cerebral palsy—his jarred motions were accentuated as he chased the ball down the field. Ophelia noticed that the parents were quite a distance away, so she was moved to help Ryan. He was a sweet boy who sometimes came over to play with Mateo.

"Leave him alone," Ophelia directed.

"Mind your bees wax," a boy named Arnold said.

Ophelia put herself between Arnold and Ryan and said to Arnold sternly, "You leave him alone."

There was something so grounded and aligned in Ophelia's tone, and she stared right into Arnold's mischievous eyes. He just shrugged and led his gang of boys away.

"Are you all right, Ryan?"

"Sure . . . thanks, Ophelia."

As Ophelia headed back to her tree sanctuary, she was startled by Chiyo standing nearby, beaming at her granddaughter. "That was a fine demonstration of compassion, dear," said Chiyo. "That reminds me of Kuan Yin."

"What is Kuan Yin, Obachan?"

"Not what, but who? Let me tell you the story . . . .

"There was a princess in ancient China who would not marry the man who her father, the king, had chosen to be her husband, and even when he sent his soldiers after her, she would not give in. Kuan Yin knew what she wanted and was willing to risk death to be true to herself. She was rescued by a magic tiger, who took her on a journey into the "world of the

Kuan Yin

dead," where she learned her true voice—the voice of compassion and love for all living beings."

"Wow! That sounds like an adventure—better than the one I was reading!" Ophelia squealed. She gave Chiyo her complete attention.

"Kuan Yin was the third daughter of an important king and queen. When the queen first became pregnant, she had a very vivid dream, in which she had swallowed the moon. Then, at the moment that Kuan Yin was about to be born, the whole kingdom shook with an earthquake, and her body was covered by heavenly clouds of rainbow colors. Despite the mystical beauty of that moment, her parents were very unhappy that she was not a boy.

"As she grew, her father planned to marry all of his daughters to important men and once again, Kuan Yin was a constant disappointment to him. She liked to dress in very simple clothes, and eat common foods, rather than to partake in the fancy feasts of the royal household. To her family Kuan Yin seemed odd and difficult. When Kuan Yin's father found a young nobleman for her to marry, she stood firmly before her father and said, 'I don't care about riches or fame. I wish to become a holy woman and to give up your world.'

"Her father answered with a firm and absolute, 'No.'

"Kuan Yin, stubborn as her father, and motivated by a true inner calling, spoke almost as firmly when she said, 'Even if you force me to work as a servant, I shall never change my mind or my attitude.'

"Although her mother pleaded with her to comply with the king's wishes, she would not give in. Kuan Yin's father gave her the dirtiest jobs in the palace, with only a little food, thinking this treatment would change her mind. Yet, she held firm to her convictions. Eventually, out of sheer exasperation, the queen sent her to the House of the White Sparrow, a training retreat for holy women. Kuan Yin loved this place and vowed never to return to the palace.

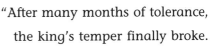

"After many months of tolerance, the king's temper finally broke. He was a man who was used to people following his orders, and he was, also, a king who did not do things in a small way! He sent a mighty force of 5,000 hand-picked ruthless soldiers to the White Sparrow with instructions to severely punish Kuan Yin. The soldiers set fire to the woods surrounding the hermitage and watched as the flames raced toward the building. Inside, pandemonium broke out, with girls and women rushing in all directions. They shrilly screamed at Kuan Yin, saying this was all her fault.

Miriam, age 11

"Terrified, she prayed to Buddha for rescue. In a moment of unusual inspiration, Kuan Yin pricked the top of her mouth and spat her own blood into the air. Instantly it transformed into vast rain clouds, which poured down upon the raging fires and put them out! The holy women and their hermitage were saved."

"Obachan, why would she DO that? Pricking her mouth like that—how weird . . . and why was her blood able to put out the fire? Was she bleeding to death?" Ophelia pleaded.

"Oh, no, Ophelia," Chiyo gently responded, "Only a few small drops from Kuan Yin magically transformed to rain clouds and put out the fire. Remember Kuan Yin is not a typical girl. Of course, girls should never cut or prick themselves like that . . . but, then again, when was the last time your father sent 5,000 soldiers to punish you?"

The Power of One

"Yeah, right," smiled Ophelia.

"You know, Ophelia-chan, these goddess stories are not always meant to be taken literally."

"What?" Ophelia looked a bit lost.

"The goddess stories are myths or legends told throughout time, to remind us about important things, like honoring one's own truth. In this story, Kuan Yin is holding firm to her convictions about becoming a holy woman, as she is called to do so on a deep level.

"Myths are also symbolic, meaning that some things that happen in them are there on purpose to teach us something. Perhaps they actually happened in that faraway time and faraway land—or perhaps, they just point us in the right direction to discover a truth for ourselves . . . . What could it symbolize, Ophelia, Kuan Yin pricking her mouth and spitting the blood in the air?"

"I'm not sure. I'll think about it. Please, Obachan, finish the story now. I want to hear about the tiger!"

"Chiyo smiled at this girl, who she so loved, and went on, "As you can imagine, this made Kuan Yin's father even angrier.

"The king sent his most trusted palace guards to seize her and to take her to the palace where she would be killed. Kuan Yin walked quietly behind the soldiers, her wrists tied with heavy ropes, as she was led to the execution square. When the executioner lifted his sword, a brilliant golden light fell all around her, and his sword shattered to pieces.

"Next, the executioner tried using a silken cord to strangle her. At that moment, a huge tiger bounded into the square, seized Kuan Yin's body in his mouth, and carried her to a mountain cave. Once the tiger put Kuan Yin on the ground, the cave dissolved around her, and her soul began its sacred journeys . . . .

"Eventually, she landed in a dark, desolate place, where the souls of the dead were tormented beyond belief. Kuan Yin began to pray for them. As they listened to her prayers, they drifted upward and disappeared, released from their torment. They were then available to be born into the bodies of babies, ready to live again.

"After some time, a huge man appeared with flames darting out of his head and eyes. It was Yen Lo Wang, ruler of the dead, overseer of those who were stuck in this underworld. He did not want the souls released and beckoned Kuan Yin to stop praying. When she would not, he escorted Kuan Yin back to the tiger's mountain cave, where she entered back into her worldly life.

"Once again, Kuan Yin began to quietly pray, and again she saw the beautiful, radiant light around her. This time, the Buddha stepped from it, carrying a peach. He said it would keep her from being hungry, or thirsty, until she attained her goal of enlightenment, the path of a true holy woman. "

Blessing The Souls

Sophia, age 12

"Where does the path of enlightenment lead, Obachan? Does it still exist today? Is it in the United States or a foreign country?" asked the wide-eyed girl.

The Power of One

"Oh . . . the path of enlightenment is not a road, like route 93," replied Chiyo, "it is a way of life. There are many aspects to this path, and Kuan Yin was exploring them all. She understood that enlightenment means learning how to be free from the human ignorance that allows people to harm each other, even in small ways, and instead to show respect for all living beings.

"Kuan Yin studied for many years. She did finally reach a point of perfect enlightenment and was ready to step fully into the brilliant light of that heightened state.

"But, I thought you said that enlightenment is not a place . . . how could she step into it?" challenged the girl.

"You're right, Ophelia, enlightenment is not an actual physical place; it is not a destination. It is a state of being. Yet, one can step into it—in much the same way as you have been learning how to shift your anger into a state of calm, a state of peace. Remember when you discovered your damaged portrait?"

"Oh, sure, I sat by Mama's koi pond."

"Well, did you feel an emotional shift? Were you able to let go of your anger at your brother and move beyond it?"

Mallie,
age 12

"Yes," Ophelia's response was immediate.

"Well, you were stepping into that place of personal peace. . . . It's kind of like that, only many times greater. When it is time, and the necessary lessons have been learned, one can step right into the magnificent brilliance of enlightenment. Enlightenment goes beyond our human understanding."

"Wow!" Ophelia stared off into the clouds.

Chiyo continued, "Right at the moment that Kuan Yin was ready to step over the threshold into enlightenment, she paused. Of all who had reached this point, none before her had ever paused to think about all who still suffered in the world—those humans who could not yet find their way, to the light of knowledge and love. They were stuck, just like the tormented souls, because of the difficulties of their lives. They had not yet discovered the path of true compassion. Kuan Yin made a vow—she would remain on Earth until every living being was enlightened. She would remain on this side of the gate of enlightenment, so that she could offer her hand to others along the path, helping them to find their way too."

"Wow!" Ophelia continued gazing off into a faraway distance. This whole idea fascinated her. How would you know if you were "called?" Would we all eventually reach this lofty place called enlightenment? Did she even want to?

"Kuan Yin forgave her father for how he had treated her. At that moment of true forgiveness, great clouds of many colors descended upon the Earth, and divine flowers rained down everywhere. When the clouds lifted, Kuan Yin became 'The Compassionate One, She Who Hears the Cries of the World.' It is believed that Kuan Yin is still here on Earth, listening and helping every one of us to reach the beautiful state of enlightenment."

"What an amazing story, Obachan."

We each can be like Kuan Yin,

when we show kindness and compassion to each other—

even to those who are seemingly undeserving."

"But Ryan is very deserving, grandmother. He is the sweetest boy."

"I know, Ophelia, but who else deserves your compassion?"

"I don't know, Obachan . . . . What am I missing?" asked Ophelia.

"When people are hurt, sometimes they act out in bitter, even hateful ways, like the father in this story. He really loved his daughter, but he was frustrated that she would not act as he desired. The king was used to getting his way, and Kuan Yin pushed him to his limits. Her decision to be a holy woman was foreign to anything that he understood. It pushed him past his tolerance, and his way of reacting was to lash out."

"Like Arnold?"

"Well, perhaps Arnold just doesn't understand Ryan. Do you think maybe he is lashing out at Ryan out of fear?"

Ophelia thought for awhile. Then she slowly and purposefully got up and made her way over to Arnold.

"Hey, Arnold, can I talk to you a minute?"

"Yeah, sure . . . . Why, are you going tell?"

"No, I'm not going to tell. I just want to talk to you."

What Ophelia didn't know was that Arnold had always looked up to her. She was so smart and seemed to have it all—friends, good grades, and the teachers liked her, too. Arnold, on the other hand, really struggled in school.

"Why did you pick on Ryan?"

"Cause he's weird."

"No, he's not, he's just different."

"But, he walks weird."

"He's got cerebral palsy. That's why he walks like that."

"Can I catch it?" Arnold asked.

"No, silly, you are born with it. Ryan goes to physical therapy every week to loosen his tight muscles, which pull his legs up like that and make it hard for him to walk. Some of his therapy is really painful—harder than working out in gym class."

"Wow, that sounds tough."

"I'm sure it isn't easy, but I know Ryan. He is a really sweet boy." Ophelia said, "He seems to do okay. At least when someone isn't hassling him!"

Ophelia looked at Arnold, this time with kindness in her eyes, as she walked away. Much later, she noticed Arnold still watching Ryan. She just knew that he was thinking about it all . . . .

Things that might remind you of Kuan Yin:
Vase with water

Statue of Kuan Yin

    Can be found at Chinese or Asian gift shops

Jade

White candle

Picture or drawing of a lotus flower

Kuan Yin picture from Internet

Kuan Yin card from goddess card deck

    Go to www.opheliasoracle.com to see our favorites!

You have passed through
two of Ophelia's Portals of Pride: As
you discover who you are and believe in
yourself, you become grounded in your own
character—the beautiful and unique, very precious "you!" Learn to trust in and believe in yourself.
Embrace your challenges and savor your successes as a
part of your "becoming." Like the caterpillar, who must
move through the many-faceted changes of the chrysalis
to find the freedom of the butterfly in flight, you, too, must
navigate the changes of this significant and exciting time
of your life.

All the possibilities of life lay before you! Experience the
delight of discovery, as you see that the world is your play-
ground. Like Ophelia, you get to "try out" many different kinds of adventures, in the quest for finding what
truly feeds your innermost desires.

One person can do extraordinary things . . . .
What is it that you have to offer?

CHAPTER 11

Cutting Through Illusion

*"When the executioner lifted his sword,
a brilliant golden light fell all around her,
and his sword shattered into pieces."*

Kuan Yin's symbolic sword of truth cuts through worldly illusion. She is able to tell what is actually true and what is not. As we mentioned in Portal Two, you, also, can develop this ability as an "inner knowing."

Your inner knowing can help guide you in the very best of ways to stay true to yourself. It is one tool to keep you on track with your own personal integrity.

Cutting through illusion is also about shifting your awareness.

Aspen, age 7

It is a way of opening beyond viewing situations through your own limited filter. Try observing through a larger scope. Imagine looking at it from all sides. The perspective is much broader than seeing from only your point of view.

Consider this example: A new movie is opening tonight and your friends are all going to see it. You really want to go. Your aunt and uncle are visiting and you haven't seen them in a couple of years. The whole family is going out to dinner and of course, you are expected to go . . . but, everybody is going to the movie.

* Given the choice—if your parents did not tell you what you had to do, what would you do? Why?
* Ask a few of your friends what they would do.

Considering all sides, instead of being focused only on getting our way, helps us to live with more insight and clarity. Do you take into consideration the feelings of others? Have you developed empathy and compassion?

Consider this:

* When both sides listen to each other openly, even arguments can shift to discussions.
* Parents will recognize you as a mature individual when you interact from this broader perspective.
* Harmony and balance are cultivated in your relationships with family and friends.

Uncovering judgments

What is a judgment? A judgment is what we think or feel about somebody else. When we hold our beliefs as facts, we keep people stuck in the little boxes that we create for them. "My cousin is a jerk. Remember that time . . . ." How long ago did that happen?

If we expect a certain action or reaction from someone, often that is the way we see them, regardless of what they bring to the experience. It is like looking through spectacles that distort our view.

If you can understand someone else's feelings, even when you don't agree with them, then you are feeling **empathy**. It is similar to the saying that we must "walk a mile in their shoes."

Did you ever move to a new school? Were you lonely? Even if you haven't had this experience yourself, can you imagine what it would be like? You can at least **empathize** with the other person.

What if you visit and help an elderly neighbor whose family lives far away? You are acting with **compassion** by showing you care.

Releasing judgements

 Take a piece of paper and write a judgment that you want to release:

I release my judgment of others based on their weight.

I release my judgment of others because of the color of their skin.

I release my judgment of others because they have a different religion than I do.

I release my judgment of other girls who hang out with a different group in school.

I release my judgment of girls who are or are not in the school band.

I release my judgment of girls who are or are not school athletes.

I release my judgment of girls who speak with an accent.

I release my judgment of girls who are or are not smart.

I release my judgment of girls who are or are not popular.

I release my judgment of girls who _____.

Repeat as needed!

After you have written as many judgments as you can think of, tear the paper up, and throw it away. You can also use dissolving paper, which can be bought from a magic store, or can be found by searching magic supplies on the Internet. Or you can write your statements on toilet paper and then have a "flushing" ritual! Use your imagination about what would help with your release.

As you destroy what you have written, say "I release this judgment, and I move toward being a compassionate person."

> "However mean your life is, meet it and live it:
> do not shun it and call it hard names . . . .
> Do not trouble yourself much to get new things, whether clothes
> or friends. Things do not change, we change."
>
> Henry David Thoreau

Yuck happens!

"Stop moping and help me carry these things to the curb for the recycle pick-up, Ophelia," her Mother said as she passed Ophelia's bedroom. "You know I have asked you twice already." Ophelia was lying on her bed staring at the ceiling.

"Mama, I just miss Obachan so much. I wish she could live here."

"I know you do; so do I, but Obachan has her own life in Japan. Perhaps we can visit her sometime, but right now I need your help."

"Can't you get Matt to help you?" Ophelia whined.

"No, he has other chores to do. We all do. Part of being a family is having to help out—you know that. I shouldn't have to ask you more than once," Toshi said in an exasperated tone.

"Okay." Ophelia got up and stomped out of her room and down the stairs. She picked up the bags of glass, plastic, and paper, loaded them into the big purple recycle container, and wheeled it out to the curb.

When she went back into the house, her mother was standing in the kitchen holding a list. "Here are a few more things I need you to do today outside, because it is supposed to rain tomorrow," she said.

Ophelia looked at her with a glare and then looked at the list. She took the list and without saying a word, went outside, making sure the door slammed in her wake. Nothing felt "right" today. She didn't want to work on releasing her anger. She just wanted to be left alone.

At school the next day, Ophelia was in a better mood. She and Marissa met before English class, and talked about who would get to be the leads of the play their class would be performing, in an assembly for the whole school. It was a comedy, and Ophelia admitted she wanted the lead girl part, Sandra. The bell rang before Marissa could answer.

As they sat in their chairs, Mr. Chapman announced that Ophelia and David would be the leads, and then he assigned parts to all the other students. Ophelia beamed at David, knowing that he was the funniest person she knew, and that it would be great to work with him.

They stayed in their chairs and started doing a read-through of the play, to get a sense of the story and how much they would have to memorize. There was a lot of nervous laughter at first, but they began to get a flow as they got used to the words. Ophelia and David had quite a few scenes together; they had excellent timing as they said their lines and waited for the laughter of the other students.

After class, Ophelia stayed to ask Mr. Chapman a question and then walked into the lunch room. She hurried over to sit next to Marissa, as she always did, but noticed that Marissa hadn't saved her a seat. The other girls at the table stopped talking when she arrived and didn't say anything to her. "Hey, Marissa, sorry I'm late. I'll catch you after school," Ophelia said cheerfully. Marissa didn't respond and just kept on eating.

Ophelia, mystified by Marissa's behavior, waited for her after school. She didn't show up. Ophelia texted, "where r u?"

There was no answer.

The Power of One

Ophelia took the bus home pondering Marissa's strange behavior, wondering what she had done to make her mad. Usually they rode the bus together every day, talking about what happened at school.

She got home and her mother had left a message on the counter, "Ophelia, please heat the chicken and vegetables leftover from last night in the microwave for you and Mateo. I have to go back to the office, and your Dad is at the gym."

"Why do I have to do EVERYTHING?" Ophelia said to no one in particular. She put down her books and turned on the TV. After dinner, she tried calling Marissa, but either her phone was off, or she wasn't answering.

At school the next day, she got snubbed by several girls. Jana called her "teacher's pet" in a snide way. Ophelia looked blankly at Jana and said, "What are you talking about?"

"Oh, Marissa told us that you were flirting with Mr. Chapman so much that he gave you the part of Sandra. She said you were bragging about how you did it."

"What are you talking about? Mr. Chapman is married and has a baby. Why would I be interested in him? Besides, I don't even know how to flirt," Ophelia said with astonishment. Why would Marissa make something up about her that was so untrue?

"It's all around 6th grade already. Sheila asked Marissa today if she wanted to be her best friend," Jana said with a superior smile.

When Ophelia got home, she wanted to talk to her mother about Marissa and the other girls and ask her what to do. But her mother was working late again, and she felt so alone. There was just no one to talk to. She didn't even want to go to school the next day; the play didn't seem so fun anymore.

By the end of the week, several of the girls were teasing Ophelia about Mr. Chapman, her new "boyfriend," and nothing she said would shut them up. Marissa was completely ignoring her, even when she tried talking to her. Her mom wasn't home in the evenings. After school, she went into her room and tried to study, but mostly she just listened to music. Everything had turned upside down so fast.

On Saturday morning, Ophelia had a stomach ache and couldn't eat breakfast. It was because she had eaten so much butterscotch pudding the night before. Her mother looked at her and said, "Ophelia, what is going on? Are you still upset about Obachan?"

"No, Mama. It's just that Marissa won't talk to me."

"Oh, honey. Girls are just that way sometimes. She'll get over it. I remember my best friend and I had a fight and didn't talk for what seemed like months, but I'll bet it wasn't more than two or three weeks."

"We didn't have a fight," Ophelia wailed. "After I got the part of Sandra in the play, she just stopped talking to me!"

"Was that the part you wanted?"

"Yes, but now I don't think I care about it. It has caused too much misery. I didn't even get a chance to tell you about it, because you haven't been here all week."

"I'm sorry. I know I didn't explain to you that I had a big project this week, a fund-raiser to help restock the library with the newest books. Our major grant was cut this year because of the economy. I am sorry that I was so consumed by my project. Tell me what is going on," Toshi said.

"Well, Marissa told everyone at school that I got the part of Sandra because I was flirting with Mr. Chapman. Why would she lie about that? Mr. Chapman is an old man!" Toshi smiled at the thought of 32-year-old Dave Chapman being considered old. "People are calling him my 'boyfriend' and teasing me, or they are completely ignoring me, like I really did something bad. Tears began to form in Ophelia's eyes. Toshi gave Ophelia a hug and held her for a bit longer than her daughter usually allowed these days.

The Power of One

"I just don't know what to do, Mama."

"The first thing you need to do is find out from Marissa what made her so mad," Toshi said. "Until we know that, it will be hard to fix things. Do you want me to talk to Mr. Chapman?"

"NO," Ophelia said loudly. "Oh, please, Mama, don't. That would be so embarrassing. How can I get Marissa to talk to me? Maybe I will just go over to her house."

Ophelia walked up the familiar steps at Marissa's house and knocked on the door. When Marissa answered, there were a few awkward moments. Ophelia decided to be direct. "What did I do to make you so mad at me?"

Marissa looked down at the ground and then invited Ophelia in. "I am so sorry, "she said. "I really wanted the part of Sandra, but I didn't want to tell you. And I felt so jealous because you got it instead of me. I thought if I made things miserable for you, you would back out, and maybe I would get the part. I really did-n't know things would go so far."

"Look, I didn't know you wanted the part. We could have talked about it. We need to be honest with each other if we're going to be friends again. And I want people to stop spreading rumors about me," Ophelia said firmly.

"I promise I'll tell everyone that the story about you and Mr. Chapman isn't true. I don't like not talking to you. You're the best friend I've ever had."

The girls hugged and headed for the kitchen for a snack. "Hey Marissa, I want to tell you a story that my grand-mother told me about Kuan Yin," Ophelia said as she grabbed an apple from a bowl on the kitchen table.

Madison,
age 11

CHAPTER 12

Appreciating Differences

Have you ever considered the ways in which people are different?

✎ Write a list of possibilities on a piece of paper or in your journal. Here are some suggestions:

- Male or female (gender)
- Christian, Jewish, Buddhist, Catholic, Hindu (religion)
- African-American, Caucasian, Asian, Native American (ethnicity)
- Physical differences such as deafness or blindness
- Personality traits such as being quiet or talkative

When we simply observe our differences
without making them "right or wrong,"
we can learn from them.

- What holidays do your friends celebrate that you may not?
- What foods are specific to their cultures?
  To their family traditions?
- Are there certain words that are unique? What does your girlfriend call her grandmother?
- What is uniquely different about you and your friends?

You can create a list of observations on your paper or in your journal.

Do you ever feel uncomfortable around someone who is different from you?

Are you ever unkind to others because they are different from you?

Has anyone ever treated you badly because of your differences?

Thinking about the Kuan Yin story, and Kuan Yin's message of compassion for others, how do you feel about people being different from one another?

It's a small, small world!

With the ease of world travel and the instant communication of the Internet, women all over the world are connecting with each other on many different levels. There is a shift going on in the world in how women care about supporting each other. We recognize that we are crucial to the peace movement, to saving the environment, and to creating a system of health care for children. For example, women in Liberia and in Kenya banded together in such strong forces that they were able to change the government leadership in their countries. Instead of being ignored, their voices were heard!

We are learning that as women of different races, cultures, and religions, we can reach out to each other. Nothing can stop this movement as more women reach out to help their sisters everywhere. You, too, can be a part of a supportive "team" for your friends and also reach out to people who are from different places or are different from you.

Giving to others does not deplete your own personal resources. As you give, you fill back up. It is a natural occurrence. As you share kind thoughts and caring actions; you receive good feelings in return. Have you ever felt the pure joy of helping another? Demonstrate the "Power of One" through your understanding, your compassion, and your appropriate caring for those around you—people, animals, and the environment.

In the U.S., there are women today who are supporting other women in developing countries by buying their goods directly at a fair market value and getting rid of costs that are added by businesses and big stores. That way, the women producing the goods, such as bracelets or bags, receive most of the money of the sale.

There are banks and organizations that give what are called "micro-loans" to poor women around the world also. These loans may be only $100 or less. A woman can buy a goat, for example, and make cheese from the milk which she can sell at the market every week. She eventually pays the money back and maybe makes enough to buy another goat. The money she earns helps to buy food, clothes, and education for her family. Visit www.kiva.org.

When women and girls are lifted out of poverty and provided an education, the whole society thrives. The poorest countries are the ones where females are not educated, honored, or allowed to create their own businesses.

One reason that Donna and Tina wanted to write this book is that they believe in a sisterhood of women that goes beyond time and space . . . . What does that mean, you might be asking?

Well, throughout time, there have been girls and women who have done amazing things. They have met challenges. They have tried new, daring experiences—sometimes changing the course of history when they did! They have laughed and shed tears. They have been young and old, rich and poor, well-remembered and unknown. Some of them may be your family ancestors; others are no blood relation. Yet, they are all family.

This is the sisterhood, and it reaches as far back as you can imagine. It stretches to the beginning of time itself. It reaches forward, too. What you do today con-nects with and impacts the girls and the women who are not yet born. Remarkable, isn't it?

It makes you realize that your actions are significant—so watch what you do, because your thoughts and your actions not only reflect on you, but are important to this sisterhood, too.

The fabulous thing is that we are never alone. In times of challenge, in times of doubt, in times when we feel lost or alone, we are not. We can always draw on the sisterhood—for inspiration, for guidance, for support.

Right now, wherever you are, stop. Close your eyes. Just breathe . . . .

Can you feel them? Can you feel the embrace of something strong and loving, reaching out to let you know that its sweet presence is there?

Trust us, it is!

The more that you learn about the ancient stories, both those stories in history and those of myth, you will feel the sisterhood more and more. You will feel the sisterhood, and you will know . . . that they are smiling on you.

For you are the present,
stepping into the future,
and we are all connected,
through time and space.

Sister Soul

Sister Soul,
    we used to know
        how to mend each other's broken bones
           with sturdy branches
           and pots of bubbling herbs and berries.

we used to know
how to mend each other's hearts
    with understanding words
    and strong arms wrapped in gentle embrace

we even used to know
how to mend an empty soul—
    gathered within the dwelling of our own wombs,
    we were reborn . . .

sitting knee to knee,
we share songs of old,
raising prayers in sweet harmony,
    in the comfort of our sisterhood,
    we overflow with sacred ceremony.

Sister Soul,
    we used to know . . .
    together—let's remember!

©Donna DeNomme 1995 / *We Moon Calendar 2007*

"Friends support each other" activity

You may already be aware of the ways that you and your friends support each other. One fun activity is one in which we get to physically demonstrate how we can work together to support each other. It is best done outside in a clear area! If you are inside, make sure that you have plenty of room.

- Begin the activity by sitting on the ground, back-to-back with your partner, with your knees bent and your elbows linked.
- All you have to do is to stand up together.
  With a little practice and co-operation, it will be pretty easy.
  Half the fun is exploring how to best accomplish this task
- You may want to try this with several partners.
- What about trying this with your family? If you do, how does doing the activity with your family differ from doing it with your friends?

"We are all interrelated" activity

To see a physical demonstration of the idea that we are all interrelated, try this fun activity:

- You will need a colorful ball of yarn.
- Gather your family or a group of friends for a conversation about anything that you want to talk about! The best themes are those that are interesting to everyone in the group.
- One person holds one end of the yarn, anchoring it by tying it around her finger or wrist.
- When someone begins to talk, the yarn is tossed to her. She

continues to share while wrapping the yarn around her wrist. When the next person shares, the yarn ball is tossed and he wraps it around his wrist while speaking.

- Continue until the conversation is done or the yarn is completely unwound.

Important! Make sure to maintain just a little slack between two speakers. Too much slack and the yarn will droop onto the floor. Too little slack will pull on sensitive wrists!

Jade, age 8

What is demonstrated, visually, is the beautiful web of communication, and the connection that naturally weaves back and forth between us.

Unraveling judgments

Ophelia headed to the mall. She was meeting Marissa and Tonya to do a little browsing for new summer clothes. Many of the styles were really cute this year, and Ophelia had high hopes for a successful shopping adventure! Mall hopping wasn't her usual form of enjoyment, but she had been saving her allowance and babysitting money for some time now, and she now had enough for a fabulous new outfit. She had even been weeding and cleaning the leaves in the Johnson's yard for the past three weeks. Her wallet was full!

Since the mall was easily accessible by bus, Ophelia had hopped on the #24 and headed mid-town. She was meeting the girls at the north entrance. She easily made the short walk from the bus stop, in the beautifully warm, early summer sunshine. Ophelia smiled as she remembered the not-too-long-ago winter storms and the long hiatus from these mall runs. When it was blustery out, she preferred to stay huddled inside with a good book or a movie. Ophelia was not one of those die-hard shoppers. You could say that she was a "fair-weather" shopper.

As Ophelia headed toward the north entrance, she noticed a small group of people off to one side. She couldn't tell what they were doing until she got fairly close. They seemed to be overly dressed for the day, with what appeared to be several layers of shirts, vests, sweaters, and pants. One of them was wearing a coat. It was way too warm a day for a coat, thought Ophelia. There was a woman and three children; one girl was about her age. An older woman was with them, too, and Ophelia imagined that she must be the grandmother. Her heart felt a twinge as she thought of her dear Obachan, and how she missed her so . . . .

The group had several bags piled nearby, partly hidden in the shrubs. As she looked at their faces, she noticed how weathered and tired they looked. Their awkward glances seemed to show that they were searching

The Power of One

for something, as they looked this way and that. What? Ophelia wondered.

She noticed the group tense as she approached, and in the next moment, she realized that it wasn't her that they feared; their faces showed a strain as they looked down the walkway, toward a man approaching. It is the security guard, Ophelia realized. Without any notice, the guard turned into The Gap several doors down, and the group began to murmur as they nervously rearranged their bags.

"I guess the security guard would have chased them off," thought Ophelia. "That must be really hard, getting shuffled around like that."

Ophelia remembered all of her recent thoughts, wondering about who she was and where she belonged. She realized that she knew where she would sleep tonight. She had parents who loved her. Ophelia knew that they loved her even in the difficult, tense family times. Even pain-in-the-neck Mateo was special to her; she loved him, too.

Yet, as she looked at this family, she could tell that they cared for each other, too. The grandmother was wiping the face of the little girl with a worn napkin, and the older kids were talking quietly between themselves. Ophelia slowly approached them.

"Hello!" she smiled.

"Hello," said the mother, somewhat cautiously.

There was a moment of awkward silence, as they all stood looking at each other. Ophelia wasn't sure what she would do next, but she continued, motivated by some unknown prodding that seemed to originate in her heart. And for some reason, pictures of Chiyo kept crossing her mind. Did her grandmother know these people? Probably not, she thought. Would her grandmother encourage her to talk with them? Ophelia didn't know that answer, but still she went on.

"Do you live around here?" Ophelia asked.

Again, they looked at each other nervously and said nothing. They just waited to see what Ophelia would do next.

"I mean no harm," said Ophelia, compassion covering her face, as her eyes reached out to console them. She knew nothing of their story, but she felt with certainty that it was not an easy one.

"We don't live around here," again the mother spoke. "We come from Lincolnville, several towns over. We came here looking for work . . . ," she paused, as her face strained, and her eyes began to fill. "We left when we lost our home . . . there isn't much left." The woman glanced in the direction of their small pile.

Ophelia's suspicions that they were homeless were confirmed. She stood for a few moments and then with certainty said to the woman, the kids, and the older woman,

"Come with me!"

They looked cautiously at each other, but quickly gathered their things and followed Ophelia around and down the side of the mall, until they arrived at the little café, which was one of Ophelia's favorites.

On the way, Ophelia texted Marissa, "meet me at the café i will explain."

The Power of One

As the bedraggled group arrived at the café, Ophelia noticed the looks from the people already gathering for an early lunch. In spite of her thoughts about herself and where she fit in, Ophelia wasn't used to people looking at her that way. Sure, sometimes she got odd glances, and people even asked out loud, "What is your ethnicity?" as they tried to figure out where her family came from. But this was different—much worse—Ophelia noticed. People were looking at this family with disgust, as if it was their fault that they were dressed the way they were. In that spark of an instant, Ophelia felt what the family must feel—embarrassed, shamed, discouraged, and kind of beaten by life. After all, they had lost their home. Honestly, Ophelia could not even imagine being homeless, and she hoped that she would never find out what that would be like . . . . She had a kitchen and a warm bed to go home to . . . and a family who loved her. Wow. Ophelia felt as if she knew exactly where her place was, where she belonged.

"Order something to eat," she said to the group.

They just stood there. The counter girl shifted anxiously from foot to foot.

"Do you eat meat?" Ophelia asked, again with a gentleness in her voice that surprised her.

Yes, the mother nodded.

"Give us five cheeseburgers, with fries, please . . . and five vanilla milk-shakes—is vanilla O.K.?"

Again the woman nodded, and Ophelia wondered if she would say yes to anything.

"O.K., vanilla it is!" Ophelia took out her pink leather wallet, the one Obachan had gotten her during her recent visit. She smiled as she counted the money from her well-guarded, long-saved stash. She had known that she was saving for something special—she couldn't have imagined that this would be it! Yet, as she handed the counter girl her money, there was no regret, no feeling of loss for another tank top or new jeans. Ophelia knew, in her heart, that this was the right thing to do, and she felt close again to her grandmother. She could feel Obachan Chiyo smiling at her, all the way from Japan.

As Ophelia beckoned the family to sit at a table by the back of the café, she noticed that her friends had come into the café by the mall entrance and were looking around for her. She waved them over, noticing the shocked and confused looks on their faces. She turned to her newest acquaintances and said, "Now, tell us your names . . . ."

The girls did not linger long. Once the burgers and fries were served, with the luscious vanilla shakes—Ophelia's favorite, by the way—the girls left. There would be no lunch with her friends for Ophelia today, and yet her belly was full with a warm, contented feeling, different from anything else she had ever known.

People are naturally generous . . . . So why do so many people seem to diregard the needs of others? Why do people appear greedy, when we are actually generous by nature?

Get this: People who don't feel good about themselves are less likely to be generous or helpful to others. Our feelings about others are a MIRROR of our feelings about ourselves.

One way to increase personal happiness is by being generous, because the person who shares with and helps others will feel better about herself as a side effect.

–Tal Ben Shahar, who teaches a course on Happiness at Harvard University.

It's easy: one good deed leads to another
and it leads to you loving you! –Tina

Alexandra, age 14

13
Helping Others:
A Path of Human Service

The Kuan Yin story that helps us to understand this Portal of Pride, is commonly told in Buddhism. Buddhism is a religion that emerged in India long, long ago. Buddhists believe that we all possess the greatest potential, and that we can achieve the highest form of insight, called enlightenment, through self-awareness and self-understanding. To achieve enlightenment, people must give up their needs for personal desire, for anger, and for ignorance. Of course, we are all "a work in progress," and so even Buddhists know that life is about becoming a more perfect being.

Buddhism was carried throughout Asia and became very important in China. Kuan Yin is well-loved in China because anyone can pray to her. She responds to the needs of ordinary people, as well as the wealthy, or the elite. She is accessible to everyone. To the Chinese, she is familiar, and she is family. She understands the fear of pain, the anguish of a lost child, or the torment of a lonely parent.

Wherever you go in China, you will find stories told by people of all ages of personal encounters with the Goddess of Compassion. Kuan Yin is a very popular feminine figure! She is the model for compassion, non-judgment, and acceptance of all. Her message to all of us is one of service to others. This message does not mean that, like Kuan Yin, you have to choose never to marry. This message does not mean that, like Kuan Yin, you must enter a hermitage and become a holy woman. We each, in our own way, can make contributions to others. All of these contributions, great and small, make a difference in the larger collective, and all are a part of the path of human service.

What have you done to contribute to others' well-being? What else could you do? Like Ophelia's experience at the mall, sometimes a simple act can go a long way to benefit another, and at the same time can compensate us in ways that are immeasurable. Be open to hearing "the call" when you are in a situation where you, too, can make a difference.

Chloe, age 14

CHAPTER 14

Kuan Yin Girl: Hannah Taylor and the Ladybug Foundation

Kuan Yin cares about all people, especially those who don't have as much as other people. No matter how plain they seem, Kuan Yin sees their brilliance! "Kindness and caring can and will change our world for the better," says Hannah Taylor, who at age eight started the Ladybug Foundation to help homeless and hungry people in Canada. Even at five years old, this compassionate young girl worried about a man that she saw eating out of a garbage can. Hannah feels so fortunate to have a safe and comfortable home and wants to reach out to help others who do not have warm food and a secure place to sleep.

She began talking with homeless people, including Rick who lives in Winnipeg. Rick cried when Hannah hugged him and told him that she cared about him. The good news about Rick is that he now has a home and a job with the help of a shelter, which received funds from the Ladybug Foundation.

Hannah and her Ladybug supporters from across Canada have created a National Red Scarf Day on January 31st that brings attention to homelessness. Thousands of Ladybug jars have cropped up in schools, businesses, and government offices to collect spare change for the homeless! Hannah herself speaks to many organizations and schools to encourage people to care for folks who are "just like you and me." With such ease and grace, Hannah embodies the essence of a Kuan Yin girl.

Hannah and the Foundation are now implementing "Make Change: The Ladybug Foundation Education Program" based on Hannah's experience. Hannah told us the program is for school kids and others to let them know that if they see a problem, even if they are "little, big, short, or tall, they can make a difference in the world for the better, by helping and caring and sharing whatever they have. And this," Hannah said, "makes my heart hopeful."

For more information about Hannah Taylor and the Ladybug Foundation, go to www.ladybugfoundation.ca.

Be a Kuan Yin Girl!

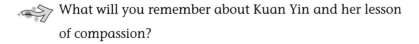

➤ What will you remember about Kuan Yin and her lesson of compassion?

➤ Did you see similarities with yourself and Kuan Yin? List your Kuan Yin qualities.

➤ What do you appreciate about people who are different from you?

➤ What judgments are you ready to let go of?

➤ Does Hannah Taylor inspire you to treat others with respect, no matter who they are?

➤ Remember that making a difference one person at a time is special, too. Where can you make a difference? Who can you help this week?

Inspiration from Kuan Yin

I, Kuan Yin, appreciate your compassionate self. You recognize the needs of others, and you value the differences in people. I see you reaching a hand out to those in need . . . . I am so proud of you and the difference that you make in the world!

make a difference

Free to Be Me!

CHAPTER 15

Unexpected Wisdom

One day after school, Ophelia and Marissa worked on a science project together. On the way home, Ophelia cut through the edge of the woods at the end of Marissa's street. A small but beautiful patch of untouched wilderness, the land had been donated by a wealthy, founding family of her town. When old lady Eliza Abernathy passed away last year, she had willed this plot in the hopes that it would remain unspoiled. Eventually, the town had plans to develop it into a wildlife preserve to protect the majestic eagles and hawks that nested here. Ophelia loved to explore in this natural sanctuary. When she was deep in the wooded wonderland, she felt as if she were miles away from the city, even though it was only a 30-acre piece of land. It is amazing how a plot of trees can "speak" to a person.

This day, Ophelia had sat down underneath a ponderosa pine tree and was snacking on some trail mix that she carried in her backpack for an energy boost. A chipmunk chirped nearby, begging for a hand-out—but Ophelia knew better! These woodland creatures needed their space to remain wild even though people were encroaching upon their homes. As cute as the little guy was, she did not want to confuse him into thinking people were convenient vending machines for snacks. She spoke gently to him, "Hey, little chipper," and left it at that.

Ophelia was a bit startled by a tall, athletic-looking woman who strode down the path. Only a few of the kids played in this spot, and she had never seen an adult there . . . . Was she an adult or what? This girl must be in college, at least. Ophelia nodded to her as she approached, and the girl smiled at her. There was something about her smile that fascinated Ophelia. What was it—a knowing, but not a smirk like when you hold a mischievous secret. There was something about her smile that was familiar. Ophelia couldn't quite put her finger on it. It reminded her of something—or someone.

"Hello, there!" said the girl.

"Oh, hi," said Ophelia.

"What are you up to?" this intriguing stranger asked Ophelia.

"I'm on my way home and I just stopped to sit for a minute . . . ."

"You mind if I join you?"

Ophelia didn't see any harm, and she was interested in who this older girl was because she noticed an unusual object slung across her shoulder. What was that? As the stranger sat down on a nearby fallen tree, Ophelia noticed that it was a bow, like the one she used sometimes in gym class, and also a quiver, which she imagined contained arrows.

"Are you hunting here?" asked Ophelia, a little concerned.

Sophia, age 12

"Oh, no, I am just passing through. I am headed south where there is an overpopulation of deer. I am needed there . . . ." the dark-haired girl said.

"Are you from around here?" Ophelia was curious and at the same time, a bit hesitant because this girl was so different from anyone she knew. Ophelia was acutely aware of her surroundings and knew the fastest way out of the woods to a nearby house where another friend lived. In her mind, she flashed on all of this just in case she needed to bolt. Of course, the girl had those arrows, Ophelia thought . . . but still her feeling was not one of danger . . . the girl felt familiar somehow and not at all threatening.

"Oh, no, Ophelia."

"How do you know my name?" Ophelia blurted!

"Ophelia, I come from another time, another place. I have come to this wood today because it is our destiny to speak. I have something to tell you . . . . I come because you have opened the portal—the portal to truth. And truth comes through many channels, many stories, many voices. You are a seeker and a seeker puts out a powerful call—one of curiosity and recep- tivity. The "call" summons forth the truth and the truth must come. It is the way. It is the destiny." And then she smiled, that smile, and Ophelia realized where she had seen it before. It was the same knowing smile of her dear grandmother. Ophelia looked deeply at the sisterly girl and con- nected with her gentle eyes. She knew in that moment that she could trust her. Besides that, these words—as weird as they were—made sense! A knowing deep within her stirred. She felt that she was a piece of something so much bigger than who she was—just one girl.

"My name is Artemis." The voice reverberated right through Ophelia.

"Artemis—that is a beautiful name . . . . You said that you are from another time . . . what did you mean?"

"I was first known in the time before the ancient Greeks, and people spoke about me for hundreds of years after that beginning time . . . . I still exist now, but most have forgotten the old stories. Now, in your time, the people are beginning to remember . . . . You, Ophelia, are curious . . . and that was how the portal was opened when you began to share the stories of the goddesses from different times and different cultures. It is your interest in those stories that called me here today! And for that, I am grateful. There is so much that has been forgotten, but not lost. The time is fertile for the old wisdom to return—all it takes is girls like you to ask the questions. There are many of us waiting for the chance to again speak. Thank you, Ophelia, for your willingness to listen . . . . " A gentle stream of steady tears streaked Artemis' face. Ophelia was taken back by this sudden emotion. This girl was so strong, and her tears beckoned Ophelia to know the importance of what was now happening.

Artemis (**AR** te miss)

Zeus (Zoose)

Leto (Lee toe)

Actaeon (**ACT** ee on)

"Tell me, Artemis. Tell me your story . . . ."

"I am the Greek Goddess of the forest and the protector of all the wild creatures. The ancient Greeks asked for my blessing before the hunt and would also say a few words of gratitude to me when they were successful. Animals were not killed for sport, but were taken to feed the people. There is honor in that practice both for the animal and for the hunter.

"My father was Zeus, the leader of the Gods on Mount Olympus, and Hera was his wife. Zeus had other lovers, and my mother, the goddess Leto, was one of them. When Hera found out that my mother, Leto, was pregnant with twins, she sent the serpent Python in pursuit of my mother and cursed her with the decree that she could only give birth where the sun didn't shine. Hera wanted to send a strong message of disapproval. It was hard for all of us, but you know Ophelia, sometimes the worst situations can have gifts hidden in the darkness. It was that way with my mother."

"What happened, Artemis? Tell me more!"

Free to Be Me

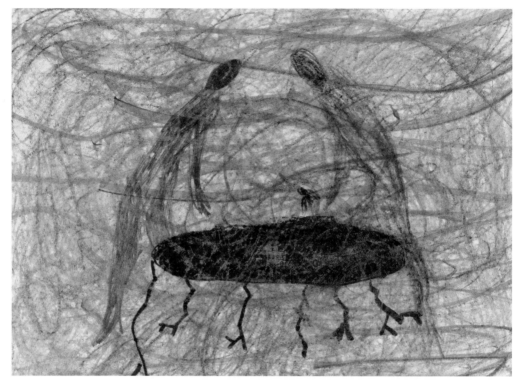

"Well, as is often the case, it was the kindness of another who brought hope to our plight . . . . The south wind befriended my mother, Leto, and sent her to an island that floated on pillars under the ocean's waters, just out of reach of the sun's rays. I was born first, and being a goddess, I was born already with some of my gifts at hand . . . although now that I ponder it, Ophelia, you humans are born with gifts, too, aren't you?"

"Well, I guess so." said Ophelia, "I don't know . . . ." She wanted Artemis to return to her own story, which seemed far more interesting than Ophelia's.

"Ophelia, you and your brother are very different in some ways and similar in others, right?"

"Yes," Ophelia answered.

"Some of that is because you were each born with your own gifts—those are special and remain yours for all of time.

"One of my gifts was that of midwifery. I was able to be my mother's midwife for the birth of my brother Apollo. Leto did not suffer any labor pains, and because of that, Greek women would ask me for help during a pregnancy to ensure a painless labor. They even named an herb after me, *Artemesia*, because it eases their labor."

"Wow! That is pretty amazing, Artemis. Is that what you do for a job?" Ophelia asked.

Artemis laughed so hard she nearly fell off the tree she was perched upon. "Not exactly, Ophelia. Goddesses are an inspiration to the people. The true power does not come from the goddess but from the people she inspires. Our stories are there as lessons to give ideas to people who create their own stories by the lives they lead. That is my job, I would say: to inspire the people so they may find their own true power.

"Let me tell you another part of my story. This might help you to understand . . . . When I was a young girl, my mother took me to visit my father, Zeus. He held me on his knee and asked me what gifts I would like from him. I always wanted to be true to my own nature, which was one of independence and inner strength. I also wanted to help others. My father recognized in me the gift of clear sight and intuitive guidance as I asked that these qualities always be maintained in me. These were pretty big requests for a young girl!"

"Why did you have to ask your father to help you with that, Artemis? My parents encourage my love of reading, and they also help me with the things I am not good at—like when I first tried to ride a horse. Isn't that just what parents do?"

"Well, yes, Ophelia. But even well-meaning parents can sometimes discourage a curious mind or a tender heart. And some of our goddess stories are about parents who were downright mean to their offspring—all for the higher purpose of the lesson the experience brought, of course . . . . So, to get back to my story, neither I nor my mother, Leto, knew how my father would react to my precocious nature. I also asked for a bow and arrow like my brother and a yellow tunic with a red hem reaching to my knees. I had one more very special thing on my list—I wanted many nymphs as my maids of honor."

"You were getting married? How old were you???" Ophelia was shocked.

"Oh, no, I never wanted to marry! 'Maids of Honor' were the nymphs who I explored the woods with and who shared my days, much like your friends."

"What's a nymph?"

Nymphs are beautiful, fairy-like, nature goddesses who have close connections with trees, rivers, and mountains. They are gentle and delightfully perky sprites . . . . I love the nymphs! They are so much fun to be with . . . . "

Ophelia was spellbound by the words of Artemis, and her vivid imagination danced in this other time and faraway place where the nature spirits worked in harmony for the good of the forest. Ophelia herself felt a kinship with all the living beings in this wooded sanctuary, and she loved to just come and sit. She could almost hear the whispering of the trees and feel the love of the ground beneath her. As foreign as this story of Artemis was, it was also so very familiar.

"I would love to visit with the nymphs," said Ophelia.

"Maybe—sometime that might come to be! Anything is possible when you believe," Artemis mused.

Ophelia suddenly remembered to ask, "What did your father do about your requests?"

"Well, Zeus gave a hearty laugh! It was big and boisterous, and it rocked the heavens. He looked at me with kindness in his eyes, and I felt totally seen and understood. In that moment I was gifted the permission to be who I am—in spite of my quirkiness! My father told me that I would be independent forever and that I possessed deep inner wisdom. I knew then that I could always trust myself."

"Wow . . . ." was all Ophelia could say.

"Yes, but later I learned that all self-assurance must be tempered with humility. I became quite proficient with my bow and arrow. I loved to hang out with my friends in the forest. Once, at the end of a very long day, I was joined by several of my closest friends near a secluded woodland cave, which had a natural arch and a lovely pool that was fed by a spring of clear water. We were so content bathing in our deliciously warm pool and basking naked in the sun."

"Eeeww . . . you were skinny dipping?" Ophelia asked with surprise.

"Oh, yes, Ophelia. Since we lived in the woods, it was so natural for us to bathe in the spring-fed pools. We didn't have a bathtub like you!"

"A young hunter, Actaeon, who was out chasing deer with his hounds, happened to stray into this remote part of the forest. He stopped when he heard our laughter. He quietly crept up behind a rock to watch. He surprised me, and my being without my bow and arrow frightened me even more. I felt exposed and vulnerable. I reached down and scooped up a handful of water, which I threw in his face, shouting, 'Now try to tell anyone how you saw us naked!'

"Immediately, from where the drops of spring water fell upon his head, the tips of stag's horns began to sprout. Then, his neck elongated, the tips of his ears became pointed, his arms and legs lengthened into spindly legs and hooves, and dappled hair covered his body. Glimpsing his face in the water, he saw that he had become a stag."

"How could that happen just from a few drops of water?" Ophelia asked in amazement.

"I am a goddess, Ophelia, and remember that my father, the great Zeus, had given me special powers to always protect myself and my

Free to Be Me

nymphs and to remain independent forever . . . . But then a terrible thing happened. When Actaeon's hounds noticed this stag nearby, they immediately gave chase, but since he couldn't shout to them, he could only flee in terror. They eventually caught him and tore him to pieces as they had been taught to do."

"Artemis! Oh, gross. How awful . . . ." Ophelia burst into tears and looked away.

"I am so sorry. I didn't intend to shock you, Ophelia, but I wanted to be truthful in how the story actually unfolded. You know, honestly, I had not thought it through. I reacted. I guess you could say I overreacted, and I didn't take the time to consider the consequences of my actions. I felt invaded. My privacy had been breached. What could I do?"

"Could you have talked to the hunter? Maybe told him to leave you alone? You hadn't even given him a warning." Ophelia offered.

"You've got a point," Artemis mused . . . . "But you know, there are no other stories such as this one, so I must say that I learned my lesson . . . and so did the hunters. They never did tread into our part of the woods again."

"Well, I wouldn't either!"

"Oh dear Ophelia, I am not to be feared. I was known as a fierce protector of girls and wild animals, and I often was able to protect by using my inner strength and nothing else. It is that skill I would like to teach you. Believe in yourself, and you will accomplish great things. Believe in yourself and trust your ability to set healthy boundaries and keep yourself safe. Speak your truth clearly and with conviction, and others will listen . . . and yes, remember my story and think your actions through. Do not harm others in the impulse of your reactions."

Although it was not yet dark, Ophelia looked up just behind Artemis and saw the rising fullness of the moon in the pending night sky. As if wrapping herself in a warm cloak, Ophelia drew close to her a new desire to claim Artemis' self-assurance. Yet, she also believed that she would need to balance that self-assurance with the gentle wisdom of humility.

Tori, age 13

Things that might remind you of Artemis:

An arrow

Anything with a crescent shape or round shape to represent the moon

Picture or figure of a deer

A wooded area

An Artemis picture from the Internet

Artemis card from goddess cards deck

Go to www.opheliasoracle.com to see our favorites!

Free to Be Me

You have passed through three of Ophelia's
Portals of Pride. You have taken a good, clear look
at who you are . . . . Have you realized just how precious
you are? There is so much beauty about you—inside and out.
You are taking the steps to develop your confidence in who you
are as an individual, so that you may gift what only you can give
through the Power of One.

The threshold you now pass is one of great opportunity. For just as
the fuzzy worm has weathered the chaos during her time of transformation and is able to embrace her joyous flight as the butterfly,
so you, too, are moving into the time of your emergence. Step forward with great anticipation as you embrace you truest self.

You are here:

Free
to Be ME!

CHAPTER 16
Personal Safety and Personal Responsibility

Artemis held her boundaries in a very dramatic, explicit manner. Actaeon went from being the aggressor, who was pursuing Artemis, to the stag who was being pursued. He experienced being literally devoured by his hounds.

People "devour" each other in many ways . . . .

- Sometimes we can be so harsh with words that "tear people up."
- Have you ever been cruel to a classmate that way?
- Or has someone been cruel to you? Or have you seen it happen?

Artemis could have changed Actaeon into a frog or some other creature. She could have imprisoned him. Instead, becoming the stag allowed the hunter, Actaeon, to experience first-hand what he did to animals and to other people. These stories are symbolic. Actaeon was ripped apart to symbolize being taken apart from his present form. He released his limited view, as the hunter, and learned what it was like to be pursued. We, too, go through many transformations, as we change and grow into the best people who we can be! It is helpful in times of difficult transition to remember that we are growing.

We are each growing and evolving into our own personal best!
Sometimes we experience "growing pains."

One important message of the Artemis story is that she instinctively feels a need to maintain her personal privacy and safety. The Goddess, Artemis, knows how to protect her personal space:

Free to Be Me

> Do you ever feel the need for privacy?

> Do you have a place where you can be alone?

> How do you hold the boundaries of your personal space?

What is your "personal space?"

We each have a personal space around us that feels comfortable depending on whom we are interacting with. Although it may seem to you like a natural human requirement, having the security of personal space around you is actually cultural in nature. In the U.S., we like to have about as much space around us as the distance of a handshake. We line up in an orderly fashion to buy tickets, to get on airplanes or buses, or to go into a concert. In other countries, traditions may be very different. Lining up may not be a requirement, and you may have to fight for your chance to get on a bus or to buy a ticket. There is a crowd, not a line, and it can be very intimidating. Americans tend to be polite in these situations and lose out until they learn the customs.

In other cultures, people also stand much closer to each other when they are speaking, and we might respond by backing up or looking away, which would make the other person think we are unfriendly. When visiting other cultures, it is important to know what acceptable behavior is. Sometimes, it is considered rude to look right in the eyes of certain elders or dignitaries. In these situations, it is important to find a balance between what is comfortable for us, and respecting the traditions of the host culture.

Even in your everyday interactions, it is beneficial to notice how far the distance is between you and another person for you to be in your comfort zone. Of course this will not be the same in every situation.

Think about the distance for you to feel comfortable and safe when standing next to:

※ A teacher or parent shouting angrily

※ A good friend sharing a secret

※ A stranger asking directions who walks up to you with a map in his hand

※ A familiar neighbor, who is returning something he borrowed and puts his arm around your shoulder

※ A panhandler asking for money

Answer these questions on a piece of paper or in your journal:

✎ Is your personal space different with a stranger than with a familiar person? In what ways?

✎ Is your personal space different depending on the other person's mood? How so?

✎ Where do you feel it in your body when your personal space is threatened? When you don't feel safe? This is important to observe. These physical symptoms can become an "early warning signal" to alert you, so that you can check further to see if someone is in fact moving into your personal space in a threatening way. We need to learn to trust the wisdom of our bodies.

An important skill: learning to set physical and energetic boundaries to keep your body safe.

✍ Do you know how to set boundaries so that your body is safe?

✍ What can you say to people who invade your personal space? Brainstorm a list.

✍ You can also list alternative actions besides speaking.

Free to Be Me

Some ideas for staying physically safe are:

⁕ Pay attention to your surroundings. Notice what is going on around you.

⁕ As we have said before, pay attention to your own "warning signal" that something is wrong. Always seek out an adult, if you feel uncomfortable, scared, or confused.

⁕ Like when Artemis first appeared on the path and Ophelia knew where she could go if she needed to, be prepared if you need a path of escape.

⁕ There is usually safety in groups, so it is best when possible to meet a friend or go together in groups to events.

⁕ Listen to warnings and advice from parents and your school.

⁕ Monitor and adjust the distance between you and those speaking to you, depending on the situation.

Nurture and take care of your physical body:

⁕ Remember to protect your hearing by not turning up the music too loud on your MP3 player, radio, or CD player.

⁕ Protect your sight and skin from harsh sunlight by wearing shades and sunscreen!

⁕ Make good choices concerning food, both with what you eat and the amount. Remember Ophelia when she drowned her sorrow in butterscotch pudding? Not such a good idea! Also remember how Ophelia carried a little trail mix for those times when she needed some fast fuel?

> It is your personal responsibility to learn ways to keep yourself physically safe.

You should never give out personal information to strangers. This includes your address, email address, phone number, school, or your parents' names. Predators can easily find out other facts about you by using these pieces of information.

People on the Internet may not be what they seem to be. It's easy for someone to give out a fake name and age. Tell an adult immediately if you come across anything that makes you feel uncomfortable, scared, or confused.

– Adapted from an article on eHow.com, a site for teen computer safety.

Safe inner space

Safe space means good personal boundaries and physical safety. It also means learning to create good, safe, internal space. If our minds are creating negative thoughts, dwelling on repetitive thoughts, or going in circles, it can sometimes be frightening! Sometimes we are overwhelmed by so much noise in the world around us that there is no time for our minds to settle down and help us create our own safe inner space. Do you always have a phone to your ear, an MP3 player on, loud music blasting, or the TV on?

You can learn to just say STOP!

Shhh!!

Shayna,
age 14

Free to Be Me

Give yourself some time to just be with yourself.

There are ways that you can learn to shift your brain energy, to improve your peaceful nature, or the quality of your thoughts.

One energy shifter

Sometimes our energy gets really sluggish, and our brain power seems mushy. Here is a great brain gym exercise to help turn your brain on! Take your fingers of both hands and rub your ears between your fingers and your thumb. Go up and down the outer edges, the ear lobe, and back up to the top. Because there are hundreds of receptors in our ears that are connected to all parts of our bodies, this activity brings our brains alive and ready to think!

As taught by Theresa "Tajali" Tolan
Co-director of the Children's Global Peace Project
www.cgpp.org

Sometimes you might feel sad, alone, scared, frustrated, or like you just don't want to be where you are right now. This is a good time to create a safe and beautiful place where you can go in your mind whenever you want to. This may be an actual place you visited that you loved, or you can make it an imaginary place that you know you would enjoy. The great thing about this place: you can go there whenever you want!

Read this guided visualization, pausing between each line to let your imagination flow.

Take two deep breaths and relax your body.

Let go of tension in your face, neck, or shoulders.

Imagine that you are walking on the Earth in a beautiful place where all the elements are present. This is a place you feel safe, where you can feel the sun on your face, a breeze at your back, and where there is a pond or a stream nearby.

Find a flat rock warmed by the sun where you decide to sit for awhile.

Listen to the birds and the insects and feel the light breeze caressing your hair.

The air smells fresh and clean, and the temperature is perfect—neither too hot nor too cold.

Now is the time to let your imagination flow! It is important that you get to design everything about this place. Landscape it as something that makes you feel safe and happy.

Are there real animals or imaginary animals? Are there little fairies? You could bring in purple foxes and yellow herons, if you wish. Just make sure that nothing in this place makes you feel scared or uncomfortable. Just sit and enjoy your safe place for 2-3 minutes.

Again, take two deep breaths and return to your outer world.

If you go to your safe place in your mind occasionally, your brain will respond by calming down and giving you a sense of comfort and well-being.

Free to Be Me

Standing up for others

On Thursday afternoon, after Ophelia had shared a pizza with the girls at Pizza Haven, she headed home. Her parents were at work, and even though they didn't call it babysitting, it was understood that Ophelia was supposed to look out for nine-year-old Mateo after school.

When she arrived home, Ophelia poked her head into Matt's room, but the room was quiet.

"Where'd he go?" thought Ophelia. "Wasn't this the day that Justin was coming over?"

Yikes! Ophelia realized that this might not have been the best day for her after-school pizza plan. She quickly scanned the rest of the house to no avail. The boys weren't there . . . and they weren't playing at the driveway basketball hoop either, because she passed that on the way into the house.

As she peered out the kitchen window, she thought she saw some movement by the lilac bush, so she dashed out the back door. Sure enough, there they were.

"Phew!" thought Ophelia. "That was a close one. I'm glad they are all right . . . . But what the heck are they up to?"

Ophelia could see the boys standing over Mama's pond. Justin tightly gripped a medium-sized rock, and as Ophelia moved closer, he lifted it over his head, poised to drop it.

"STOP!" screamed Ophelia.

"Love everyone and every creature of nature."

Shayna age 14

Justin and Matt almost jumped out of their skins because they hadn't seen Ophelia come home. As she came closer, Ophelia realized why Justin had this rock in his hands. Thank goodness she had interrupted them when she did. There peeking out of the rocks around the backyard pond was a small pale grey bull snake. He had black splotches on his back. The poor little guy thought that he was safe because his little  head was hidden between the rocks. Yet, there he was with his body fully exposed—almost victim to Justin's forceful rock bash.

"What are you guys *do-ing?*" Ophelia scolded.

"It's a snake!" said Matt.

"Well, I can see that, dorkhead, but what are you doing to that snake?"

"We're gonna smash it!" proclaimed Justin.

"Oh, no, YOU ARE NOT," said Ophelia firmly.

"But what if he bites us?" asked Justin, looking kind of scared, but mostly wanting to justify his actions.

"Oh, I see," said Ophelia, "so you are going to smash him just in case he might bite you. What if I make you go home just in case you misbehave . . . . Ooops! Too late! You already have!"

Ophelia glanced at the little guy still lying between the rocks, his body fully exposed, oblivious to the whole scene unfolding. He had no idea how close he had just come . . . .

"Why do you care about that old snake anyway?" asked Matt.

"It isn't an old snake, it's just a baby. What did he ever do to you? Do you just go around hurting things?" Ophelia glared at the boys. She was a bit shocked at her brother's behavior. Usually he was a pretty good kid.

"Not only that, but we have a responsibility to protect wildlife. Unless

Free to Be Me

there is a definite danger to us, no living thing should be harmed. When one species is hurt, that loss affects other species. The natural balance can be upset."

"All from one little snake?" challenged Justin.

"Well, kinda," Ophelia softened as she realized that the boys were paying attention, "Earth Guardianship is what my friend, Artemis, calls it . . . . Do you remember when we uncovered the pond this year, Matt? There was that huge five-foot snake under the tarp—she didn't bite any of us even though we disturbed her sleep. Well, this little guy is probably her baby . . . . And I suspect that he thinks he's safe with his head stuck between those two rocks. Don't you think that's kind of mean to just smush him? His mother didn't bother us—why bother him?" Ophelia went on because now she had a captive audience.

"We, as Earth Guardians, need to protect the Earth and its animals, plants, too, and try to help conserve our resources."

"I know: reduce, reuse, and recycle!" chimed in Justin.

"Yes, you've got it!" praised Ophelia.

"Earth Guardianship goes beyond the three "R's" to the understanding that all the Earth beings are really a part of our family, too. Treat them with the same consideration. Sure, you can't go up and pet a mountain lion. You have to be smart about it. But you don't have to bother the mountain lion either. Earth guardianship means realizing that we don't need to dominate the land; we share this Earth . . . ."

"Hey, Ophelia, who is this Artemis? I never saw her with you. Is she a high school kid?" asked Matt.

Now, Ophelia had that knowing smile. "Let me tell you her story . . . ." she said.

Earth Guardianship

Lynn, age 10

Artemis is considered a guardian of the Earth and her creatures. Because of our current crucial environmental issues, such as deforestation, climate change, endangered species, and loss of productive land to development, there are many ways we, too, can respond as Earth Guardians.

We can shift any harmful practices to positive ones that contribute to helping the Earth. Are you willing to join Ophelia and Artemis by being Earth Guardians by protecting our Earth?

Here are some ideas:

☑ Plant a tree, like the Tree Musketeers (see page 33). Start with your yard or a friend's yard. If you live in an apartment or condo, get permission from a park to plant your tree.

☑ Join an organization that works to protect animals and their habitats.

☑ Reduce your family's carbon footprint. One of the concerns that scientists have is how much carbon dioxide is being released into the air. It is a major cause of global climate change. You can figure how much carbon dioxide your family emits and how you can reduce it. Check out the following websites to calculate your "carbon footprint."

www.nature.org/initiatives/climatechange/calculator

www.epa.gov/climatechange/emissions/ind_calculator.html

☑ Measure how much trash goes to the landfill. Count the number of trash barrels you fill up every week. Have you ever noticed how much "stuff" your family throws away? Then work together to cut back on trash.

☑ Is there a recycling center in your town?

☑ Can you donate some things to a resale organization that could be used again?

☑ Could you make some money by having a garage or yard sale?

☑ Can you buy things that have less packaging?

☑ Can you get cloth bags to take to the grocery store or other shops, so you don't come home with lots of plastic or paper bags? (Some stores have even stopped giving out bags. This practice has been in effect for years in other countries.)

☑ Get together a group of friends to start a recycling club at your school.

☑ Brainstorm with your friends to find what you are passionate about and what would have the most success. Girls are smart and creative. We're sure that you can think of other things to do.

By being conscious of what we do every day,
each of us can be a better Earth Guardian.

Aspen, age 7

Free to Be Me

Other things I can do to protect the earth:

- Turn off lights when no one is in the room.

- Add a layer of clothes in winter and shed one in summer to reduce my family's use of heat or air conditioning.

- Don't let water run when brushing teeth or washing hands.

- Trade things with my friends so we each get something "new."

- Ride a bike or walk whenever I can.

- Think of several alternatives instead of throwing something away.

A gift to you from nature!

Have you ever looked inside the branch of a cottonwood tree? Choose a dry branch from the ground under a cottonwood tree. Snap it right at the place where a few tiny rings encircle the branch and look inside. What do you see? A tiny imprint of a star will be peeking out at you!

Q: Explain one of the processes by which water can be made safe to drink.

A. Flirtation makes water safe to drink because it removes large pollutants like grit, sand, dead sheep, and canoeists.

Answer on a science exam

Madison, age 12

Anna, age 10

Free to Be Me

Morning Blessing

by Tina Proctor©

My feet stretch as the blood starts coursing.

I touch the ground and send the roots into the Earth

Knowing her nourishment will sustain me this day.

The movement of my arms is arousing.

I stretch toward the sky and send my branches to the sun

Knowing the fire will fuel my growth and creation.

My body bends and curls in response to the wind.

I honor the four directions with a gentle bow

Knowing the air will grace me with its power.

My skin is softened by the morning mist.

I breathe the
moistness deeply
into my lungs

Knowing the water will
refresh my soul.

May all the Earthly
creatures be blessed this day

by the sacred dance of
earth, fire, air and water.

What is in Your "Backpack?"

Discovering what you want

When you pack a backpack, you can choose many different things to put into it. The first step is to decide what you want. The contents of your backpack would look different if you were going hiking for a day or if you were going to school. The same is true for your symbolic "backpack."

Your backpack contains the skills, the capabilities, the gifts, and even the challenges that make you the individual girl that you are.

Shayna, age 14

So, first is to ponder, what do I want? This is not necessarily what your teachers, your friends, or your parents want for you, but what do you want for yourself? This is not necessarily what you want to go to study in college or what you want to do eventually for a career.

This is about the quality of your life—the pursuits that bring you joy and satisfaction. Some girls we know really respond to nature. Like Ophelia and Artemis, they feel at home in the woods. Part of packing their backpack might include deciding to find ways to spend time in the outdoors, as much as possible. Other girls prefer to dress really nicely. For them, the backpack might include ways to primp!

Free to Be Me

Ask yourself these questions. Write your thoughts in a notebook or journal:

- ✎ What do I like to do with my spare time?
- ✎ Do I prefer to hang out in groups or with just one friend?
- ✎ Do I like spending time alone?
- ✎ Do we spend time together as a family?
- ✎ What are the most important activities to me?
- ✎ When do I feel like I am having fun?

> "Whatever one loves, is."
>
> Sappho (female Greek poet)
>
> "Let the beauty of what you love, be what you do."
>
> Rumi (male Persian poet)

Do you have what you need?

All individuals have certain basic human needs (see box on page 156). When those basic needs are met, you have the freedom to pursue your personal needs.

Once you know what your preferences are, then you can assess whether or not you already have what you need. This is how you pack your own backpack. Many times we carry within us the ability to do what we want to do. Sometimes we may not even know it! Donna says, "One girl who I knew would never sing with us when we would sing with the radio. One night, years later, I walked into a nightclub, and there she was with a microphone in her hand and a full band behind her. Who would have known!"

You can make the best choices for yourself. When you acknowledge what it is you truly want, then you can draw in the support you need to help you develop in ways that are in keeping with your truest desires. In some cases, you may have to wait to put a plan fully into action, but you can still hone your skills to reach your goal.

For example, if you want to visit the moon, you may not be able to do so next week, but you could buy a telescope and watch the moon and all of its changes. You could study hard in science, develop yourself on the physical level, and read first-person accounts of what it is like on the moon—one day, perhaps you, too, could be an astronaut. If you enjoy music, there might be many ways to pack your backpack. Donna loves to listen to music, but she does not play a musical instrument. Does your backpack contain piano lessons?

This backpack carries the understanding that it is you, the individual, who does the packing. People are capable of making choices for themselves. Even very young children enjoy being asked to choose—this toy or that one? It is a part of our human nature to want to make some decisions for ourselves. Even though there are still some areas where your parents or your teachers will help, there are other decisions you can make. Ask your parents to point out when and where you can spread your wings by making your own decisions.

Shayna, age 14

Free to Be Me

The 7 Universal Needs

When we talk to children about universal peace, we tell them that everyone needs:

Air

Water

Food

Shelter

Safety

To be loved and to love

To belong

We each have a special gift to share with the world. When we recognize that we all have the same universal needs, that awareness helps us go into our hearts, and to listen to how we may meet those universal needs for everyone.

As taught by Theresa "Tajali" Tolan
Co-director of the Children's Global Peace Project
www.cgpp.org

Material originally excerpted from No-Fault Classroom by Sura Hart and Victoria Kindle Hodson

Turning your wishes into intentions

Assuming that your basic needs are met, and that you have identified what it is you want—now what?

> Take your wishes and "amp them up"
> by turning them into Purposeful Intentions

If you hold a secret desire to become a dancer or even just to experience dance, what can you do with that desire?

You can pack your backpack with all things dance-related. You can watch movies about dance, research possibilities on the Internet, get library books about dance, and check into schools in your area. Some offer inexpensive sample classes. You might even find a free intro session!

You can turn your interest into an official intention, by making a clear, focused statement about it. Perhaps, something like this:

I, _____, want to explore the world of dance. I dance whenever I can—even when no one else is around. I notice the potential of dance wherever I look. Life itself is a dance, and I embrace it wholeheartedly, as I dance to my heart's desire!

"Trial and Error" discovery

Ophelia noticed that Actaeon was not given a warning when he came upon Artemis and her nymphs bathing. Did he mean to be disrespectful? Ophelia called Artemis on how Actaeon was punished so severely. As Artemis mentioned, in her defense, there are no other stories of Artemis reacting this way to an intruder in her woods.

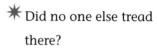 Did no one else tread there?

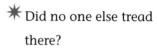 Or did she learn from this experience and choose to behave in a different way?

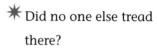 Are there times that you have learned from your "mistakes?"

Sometimes certain things will be in your symbolic backpack and then, like rotten fruit, they will be tossed aside and replaced with something fresh and new.

Madison, age 11

mistakes

mistakes are made.

Big mistakes.

just one, is all it takes.

one mistake . . .

great pains

and great aches.

mistakes are made.

great mistakes.

just one mistake is all it takes.

one mistake . . .

a different life . . .

an altered fate.

mistakes are made.

Big mistakes.

just one mistakes is all it takes.

one mistake.

we've all made one . . .

yet you've made two . . .

i've made more . . .

more than a few.

mistakes are made.

great mistakes.

Big mistakes.

mistakes are made.

Madelyn, age 16

When we give ourselves permission to try out different things—to pack our backpacks in different ways—we sometimes discover parts of ourselves that might seem to be in contrast with one other.

Artemis was considered by the Greeks to be the protector of wild creatures, and also the goddess of the hunt. How do these two actions fit together? Do you have aspects, or qualities, of who you are that seem to be opposites, but are both a part of you?

For example, one girl we know is shy and often quiet, but she is also the president of her debate club. Another girl is very bright and loves to read, but she often doesn't complete her homework, because she has her nose in a different book!

It is helpful to look at all the aspects of who we are, as individuals. Like the rainbow, we don't have to only express one part of who we are—there are many possibilities. The task is to find the perfect combination that balances our personality in the ways that we choose to express.

Interdependence

You've probably heard the saying, "No man is an island." Well, "no woman is an island" either . . . . As strong and independent as you can be, you will still always have a healthy need for inter-dependence.

Your life will intersect

with others,

by choice and

by circumstance.

Seize the adventure of life!

Even those people

who challenge

or irritate you

have something to offer . . .

and some people
will truly warm your
heart!

Donna DeNomme

Freedom

My dirty, blackened
feet swing me forward
down the street.
Unconsciously evading gravel
and cracks
and high-heeled women.
I can hear the steady
thump, thump as my heels
hit the cobbled pavement.
Minty freshness sitting on
my lips and
my education resting
on my shoulders.
I can feel freedom
seep through my soles
and to my fingers and nose.
My toes skim the
warm blacktop,
face raised to the
setting sun, exalting
in the beauty in and out of my body.
My freedom is constructing
wings of hope and love.
Lifting me to the
highest star in the sky.
My hands touch silver
spoons full of hope
and wine glasses full of
tinkling fairy bells;
washing down
my back and legs. Giggling
sweet melodies to my heart.
I will sew them into my soul.
My lace and my heart, weaving tapestries
of ashes and fire and bells. I will sprinkle
it with shoe-studded diamonds.
Travel on, my freedom, you will be great.

JJ Greenwood, age 16

The Greeks felt the presence of their gods everywhere and depicted them in idealized human form. Because the Greeks had an alphabet and wrote about their deities, we know a lot about them. In the beginning was a great void called Chaos. The Elder Gods, called the Titans, emerged from Chaos. Cronos, leader of the Titans, was father to Zeus, who led the next generation of deities called the Olympians. With Mt. Olympus as their home, the main goddesses were Athena, Artemis, Hera, Demeter, and Aphrodite.

Artemis emerged within Greek mythology as a goddess who was given permission by Zeus not to marry, but to experience freedom as the protector of wild creatures and supporter of women and girls.

In Athens, fathers arranged marriages for their adolescent daughters, who then came under the control of their husbands. In Sparta, however, where the admiration of Artemis was strong, women were extremely free and independent. They were given the high standing of being holy priestesses. All women and young girls, married or not, could spend time together in ecstatic dances dedicated to the goddess. Artemis, then and now, provides a model for independence, self-reliance, courage, and her deep honoring of the natural world.

Free to Be Me

Artemis told Ophelia that the ancient Greeks believed their gods and goddesses to be all-powerful. Artemis was quite revered because the ancient Greeks believed that everything came from the gods and the goddesses. Humans had to make proper use of what the gods provided . . . .

Alexandra, age 14

"In my earliest time, Ophelia, the people had beautiful ways to show respect for me through their sacred art, dance, and ceremony."

"That sounds nice," said Ophelia.

"It was lovely," smiled Artemis, "and yet, it was exciting, as time evolved, to see that the Greeks began to use my stories to understand the power and the wisdom of women. Women were given more and more personal freedom. They were allowed to make some of their own personal choices."

"Like what?" Ophelia asked.

"Like choosing who they would marry. And women were allowed to decide how they would celebrate their special feminine days."

"What's a 'feminine day'?" Ophelia was lost in this part of the story.

"There were lots of times that were special to women and girls, like when girls were on the threshold of becoming women. In Brauron, girls who hadn't yet menstruated held rituals as young bears, and brought the power of me as the 'bear mother' into themselves. From that time forward, whenever they felt alone or needed help, they would look to the night sky and summon the memory of their connection with me, simply by gazing upon the constellation of the Great Bear. You know this as the Big Dipper."

"I see." Ophelia was catching up. She, too, experienced some special "girl time" in her family, like her special outings with Obachan Chiyo.

"Ages ago, the people consulted oracles for guidance. These oracles, who were gifted people were believed to be in communication with me directly."

"Communication? You mean they talked with you?" asked Ophelia.

"Yes." answered Artemis.

"But I'm talking with you right now," piped in Ophelia, somewhat confused again.

"I know, dear Ophelia—this is the great blessing of your time. People no longer need to seek out an oracle to communicate with us. You are learning to recognize and activate that power which is within you."

"We are?"

"Yes, and you are one of the first, but there are many more who will follow. The paths have been opened, and the communication is clear. All one has to do is ask and then listen."

"I can see you and talk with you whenever I want?" Ophelia asked excitedly.

"Well, not exactly, but my messages are always there . . . as are the messages of the others. They are just waiting to be picked."

"What will we do with all of these messages?"

"Well, you know, Ophelia, the most important messages come from your own wisdom. Sometimes our stories can inspire your own wisdom to step forward. You really no longer need oracles . . . ."

"Wow!" this seemed important, Ophelia mused.

"Well, actually, you do. You need one oracle . . . the one that is always within you. You, my dear, and each and every girl, every woman, is the truest oracle for herself. You can be open to support and guidance from others, but you must always check it with your inner wisdom to refine its meaning.

"Of course, your parents still help you a lot, right now, but in the next few years that will greatly shift. You must practice finding your own inner knowing, listening to it, and learning its meaning, so when the time is ripe, you will be able to step forward strong and wise. Do you understand?"

Ophelia nodded, with her eyes wide with wonder.

"This is a personal freedom like never before experienced. With it comes the responsibility of a life well-lived. You must do your very best, to be the best girl you can be, and to grow into the fine woman who is inside of you."

Again Ophelia did not speak, but only nodded.

"This is truly a significant and powerful time for women . . . . It is a time for bringing forth the natural balance—between women and men. It is a time of bringing forth the balance between independence and interdependence. You are fortunate to be alive during this time, Ophelia. This is an exciting time for all people . . . ."

CHAPTER 19

Artemis Girl: Casey Clayton and Girls with a Voice

Artemis reminds us to take care of and strengthen our bodies. She is also the protector of animals and girls. Even when she was in middle school, Casey Clayton remembers wanting to help other kids. But she was the kid that others made fun of, and then when she was a freshman in a new school, she was a self-proclaimed "slacker." Did that stop Casey? No! Because of her athletic ability and a natural affinity for running inherited from her mother, Casey was asked to step into a leadership role with her team. As Casey recounts, "even though I didn't practice, I was super good and went to state as a freshman." As captain of the Sprint Team, Casey was like a fish to water. Receiving awards like "All-Over-Athlete" and "Most Valuable Player" has come easily to Casey, but the most gratifying piece has been the team spirit that she has found in her career as a runner. "I love relays and getting to run with the team. Whether or not we win the race, it's fun to work with them!"

After attending a week-long, school-sponsored teen motivational camp, Casey had an inspiration to help other girls. When she shared her idea with her father and he supported her, Casey "sprung" into action! She posted a bulletin on MySpace and received a warm response to her idea. With the help of the "coolest teacher in school," Miss Owens, Girls with a Voice was born. The purpose of the group was for girls to get to know each other beyond the small clique groups that have a tendency to form in schools. "You find some people you can be yourself around and it gives you encouragement." Deep friendships have formed, and some of the kids have even "lightened quite a bit."

Girls with a Voice was inspired less than a year ago and is already expanding into another location. At this point the girls "are pretty much running the group themselves." Casey also has plans to develop a motivational program for kids in middle school to help them actively engage sooner and to help nurture their self-confidence.

Casey Clayton—athlete, mentor, and teen leader—is our Artemis Girl because she embodies the qualities of confidence and the courage to be bold in the face of challenge. Shy new kid in freshman year? "I got to make my own name for myself by doing what makes me—me! I want to be known for me!"

For more information, you can visit the Girls with a Voice Website at www.donthideyou.com

Be an Artemis Girl!

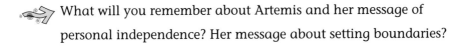 What will you remember about Artemis and her message of personal independence? Her message about setting boundaries?

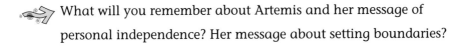 Did you see similarities with yourself and Artemis? List your Artemis qualities.

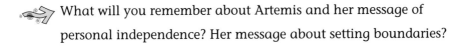 In what ways are you an Earth Guardian?

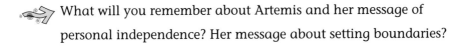 How did Artemis (or our Artemis goddess girl, Casey Clayton) inspire you?

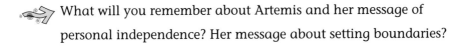 Do you already have what you need in your "backpack?" If not, how could you add to it?

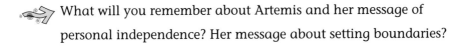 How can you be an Artemis Girl?

Inspiration from Artemis

I, Artemis, recognize your many talents. May you believe in the strength of your own body, and the strength of your own convictions. As you appreciate your independent spirit, know also that you belong to a community of women who support you, and nothing can get in your way! Believe in who you are and what you can do!

strength

Free to Be Me

The Winds of Change

CHAPTER

20

Gathering Forces

*"Children are the living messages that
we send into a time that we will never see . . . .
What message are we sending? We whisper
to the wind, and our words reach out to find a soft,
receptive spot to land. It is there that those words take
shape and create into form . . . . "* Donna

Ophelia's arms were covered with flour. She was in the midst of learn-ing the fine art of making flour tortillas, which would be filled with the most delicious chicken and beef mixed with cheese and peppers. Ophelia was learning the "secret ingredients" for Aunt Marisol's legendary dishes, many of them brought to the U.S. from Mexico, where Marisol's father had a popular café by the beach.

Ophelia loved cooking with her auntie. Not only did she enjoy being around all the good food, but the richness of their conversation was like eating desert all day long!

The window in the dining room rattled as a strong wind blew through the ranch. Ophelia watched outside as Uncle Fredo and Mateo ran after the empty feed bucket and some gloves, which had been carried off by the strong force.

Ophelia really loved the wind. She felt a special kinship with it—totally at home with the movement and the sound, even when, like today, the wind was a strong force to be reckoned with. What was that about? She wondered where this family-like feeling for the wind came from . . . .

"What are you working on in school, mi sobrina?" Marisol asked her niece.

"Oh, nothing that is exciting right now. We are just getting ready for our finals in a couple of weeks." Ophelia answered. As much as she loved school, Ophelia was looking forward to her summer break. She began to daydream about what her summer days might be like, when she realized that she did have something with her that she wanted to show Aunt Marisol. Ophelia rinsed her hands all the way up to her elbows, removing most of the fine white flour.

"I wanted to show you what I've been playing around with since Obachan Chiyo went back to Japan," Ophelia disappeared into the other room to get her backpack. She dug around, emerging with a sketch pad. She found Aunt Marisol in the dining room picking out some special dishes for tonight's meal. Ophelia set the sketch pad down on the large maple table. That table was auntie's pride and joy, as it had been handed down in her family and brought from Mexico, just like the recipes! Ophelia opened the sketch pad and slowly flipped from page to page, displaying simple, yet beautiful brush strokes.

"Oh, how graceful those are," remarked Marisol, "Did you learn that in art class?"

"No, Obachan showed me," Ophelia dug around for something else,

Stone
川
岩
石

and this time offered her aunt a small book, which had the "The Art of Kanji" written on the cover.

"I've been experimenting with these Japanese symbols. It's kind of fun!"

". . . . and so very beautiful," chimed in Marisol.

"This one's my favorite so far." Ophelia pointed to the one that was labeled "light."

光 Light

"I draw one each day, and it's kind of funny, but the word seems to follow me through my day . . . . I've been careful since I figured that out. I focus on the positive ones! Like the day I drew 'health.' Two of my best friends went home with the stomach flu, and I lucked out and didn't get it."

"What a coincidence!" Marisol responded.

"I thought so, too," Ophelia joined in.

"Well, it never hurts to be positive," recommended Marisol. "My mother used to say that what goes around, comes around."

"What?" Ophelia was lost on that one. Just as she spoke her confusion, the window right beside her began to rattle, making quite a racket. She jumped in its direction, practically feeling the intensity of the wind inside as well as out, as it seemed to blow right through her.

"Oh, dear, I must get Fredo to fix that window!" Marisol stuck a folded up napkin in the crack, bracing the frame.

風 Wind

Ophelia stared back at the wind whipping this way and that, as she recognized herself in that natural dance. "With the intensity of how everything has been lately," she thought, "there has been a great whirlwind inside of me, too. Sometimes it blows everything around like that stuff in the corral that Matt and Uncle Fredo were chasing. Sometimes it just feels as if it's gathering forces that are inside of me." Ophelia giggled as she realized that she didn't quite understand what she was thinking! But it did seem to make sense somehow. She could feel

Winds of Change

an energy, a great force, gathering inside of her, almost like it was leading up to something. "What could it be leading up to?" she wondered.

Aunt Marisol broke in, "You sure got the daydreams today, don't ya, girl? You want to take a little break?"

"Oh, no, Aunt Marisol, tell me more about what your mama used to say."

"Oh, dear, in all the excitement, I'd almost forgotten. She used to say what goes around, comes around. What that means is what you put out there in life has a tendency to come back to you. So, if you put out fun and laughter, you get that kind of day back. And if you put out mean and grouchy, well, you attract that back, too. It's kind of like a boomerang."

Ophelia understood what Aunt Marisol meant because Uncle Fredo liked to throw the boomerang, and then impress the kids by catching it when it returned. No matter how hard he threw it, that boomerang always spun around and then came back to him.

"Ah-ha!" confirmed Ophelia.

The two of them laughed together as they headed back to the kitchen to finish cooking the special flan for tonight. Ophelia had new warmth, deep within her belly. In spite of the great-force winds, inside and out, there was also a feeling of deep contentment—like everything was alright, unfolding perfectly within some unknown plan. Sure, Ophelia still had lots of questions. That was just the kind of girl that she was! Even with all of those questions, she was certain about one thing. She realized that people, and the families that they lived in, came in many shapes and many forms. The common thread was love. Ophelia had realized the importance of the love, which seemed to bind everything together. She was more aware of how people treated each other and the ways in which they expressed their appreciation. Even though she still didn't have all the answers, Ophelia had begun to feel at home in her own skin—at least for today!

My heart is like the clouds today:
layers of indecision, confusion, hope, excitement.
I look west to see the chill sun
setting behind the dark silhouette of mountains.
Grey clouds stand out as sharply as a shadow
against the pale haze brightened by the sun's rays.
A glint of sapphire flashes
between the clutter of the awaiting storm.
I watch, in awe, as the dark, skeletal features
of long dead trees thrust into the air,
an intense contrast to the stagnant steel sky.
I feel the warmth of the breeze caressing my cheek,
a contradiction to the foreboding, clouded heavens.
The wind tosses my hair lightly,
a small gust of brown curls.
The leaves dance about my feet in the meandering wind,
sounding like my heart at the sight of such beauty.
I am these clouds; this is my soul. . . .

JJ Greenwood, age 13

Winds of Change

Who is the oracle?

In ancient times, an oracle was a person who listened to the questions that people had and gave them answers. The people believed that the answers came from the gods and goddesses, speaking through the oracles. The oracles were recognized for speaking the highest wisdom. They were given ultimate authority in many circumstances.

In Ophelia's modern world, she seeks out the wisdom of others, too, like her grandmother Chiyo and Aunt Marisol. Some of her decisions are still decided by her parents, although more and more, her parents are asking for her opinion when making decisions that affect her.

Most importantly in Ophelia's story is that she discovers the truest oracle. Ophelia learns to listen to her own intuition. She learns to be steady in what she knows is her innermost truth, and at the same time open to the help and support of others. Does this mean that Ophelia always does everything right? Of course not, none of us do. But as a 12-year-old, she is discovering an inner wisdom that she didn't know she had. Ophelia has a lot more to learn about life, but she has a solid start because she knows that she can trust herself. Ophelia doesn't have to look far for her oracle. If she only takes the time to honestly listen to her inner guidance, she can find many of her answers, right inside of her. Ophelia has found her oracle!

Crossing the threshold

You have crossed the threshold of five portals.
Portals are doorways to places of new adventures.
They are openings to vast new discoveries about you,
about the world you live in,
and about things beyond your imagination.
Our wish is that you delight in this journey—
for the most important journey that you will ever take
is the one within yourself.

It has been our privilege and our joy
to share this part of your adventure.

You carry these portals and the wisdom they hold with you . . . .
Journey well!

THE FIRST PORTAL OF PRIDE:

Who is That Girl in the Mirror?

✴ Being open to honest observation, and honest
assessment of yourself

  ✴ Seeing your physical self. Taking pride
in your physical body.

    ✴ Recognizing your beauty—inside and out!

    ✴ Being aware of your emotional self

    ✴ Learning skills to acknowledge and deal
with your own emotions

   ✴ Knowing your connection with all of life

  ✴ Taking responsibility for our planet

 ✴ Who is that girl in the mirror?

Let your Smile Shine Bright As the Sun!

THE SECOND PORTAL OF PRIDE:

Believing in Yourself

✴ Taking the time to know yourself

 ✴ Recognizing your true character

  ✴ Developing confidence in yourself

   ✴ Believing in yourself, even when
others doubt you

    ✴ Being brave

    ✴ Listening to your own sense of knowing

   ✴ Understanding and learning how to
deal with your own doubt

 ✴ Believing in yourself

THE THIRD PORTAL OF PRIDE:
The Power of One

Heart

Jena, age 12

✳ Acknowledging that spiritual "holy" part of yourself

✳ Finding your own way to honor a greater Divine Presence in your life

✳ Having compassion for all living beings

✳ Reaching a hand to others

✳ Staying true to your own inner truth

✳ Honoring the sisterhood of girls and women

✳ The power of one

THE FOURTH PORTAL OF PRIDE:
Free to Be Me!

Sohpia, age 12

✳ Being strong and resilient

✳ Keeping yourself safe physically

✳ Keeping yourself safe emotionally

✳ Packing your own backpack. What's in yours?

✳ Offering your wisdom to others

✳ Being an Earth guardian

✳ Being in the community of girls and women

✳ Independence and interdependence

✳ Free to Be Me

FIFTH PORTAL OF PRIDE:

The Winds of Change

✳ Being self-aware

✳ Gathering the forces inside and out

✳ Knowing where to get support when you need it

✳ Trusting your own natural rhythms

✳ Trusting in the wisdom of your own process

✳ Opening to your own greatness, which is yet to come!

✳ The winds of change

"If stories come to you, care for them.
And learn to give them anywhere they are needed.
Sometimes a person needs a story
more than food to stay alive."

Barry Lopez, *Crow and Weasel*

Ophelia was so taken by the honoring stories of women that she often heard them in her head—even when no one else was there telling her those stories! The messages seemed to dance around in her head, waiting for a time when Ophelia needed them, and then, poof! They appeared, just in time for the perfect inspiration . . . .

Once they appeared when Sara Beth was teasing her about "still being a little girl." Many of her friends, like Sara Beth, had already gotten their menstrual periods. So far Ophelia had not. On this particular day, Sara Beth found great pleasure in taunting Ophelia.

Ophelia retreated to the girls' room. In the privacy of the stall, tears quietly fell into her lap as she wondered why it was taking so long for her body to shift into that next step. She had many of the signs they had learned about in health class—she had experienced a growth spurt, her breasts had become fuller, and she even had some hair growing down there. Why was her body failing her?

Ophelia returned to class. The rest of the day was a bit of a blur because her mind was focused on thoughts about her body. It was a good body—strong and resilient. She had always been good at sports. They came easy to her. So why was her body so slow to create that stuff she had learned about that told you that you were finally a girl in her prime, moving into womanhood? All day, Ophelia walked around in a dark haze of disappointment. This space was a non-productive one at that, because how do you possibly make your body do something?

All she could do was wait . . . .

It was then that Ophelia remembered the story that Artemis had told her that mystical night in the woods. With the fullness of the rising moon behind her, beautiful and strong Artemis was a sight that Ophelia would never forget.

As the two of them lingered in their last precious moments together, Artemis spoke in a knowing tone, "Ophelia, I feel moved to share with you about my friend, Rhiannon, who . . . . "

"I know Rhiannon," Ophelia broke in. "Well . . . I don't KNOW Rhiannon, but I know of her—the horsewoman, Colleen, told me her story."

"Ah, perfect, then you know that Rhiannon is a shapeshifter."

"A shapeshifter? What is a shapeshifter?" Ophelia liked the way it sounded, so she spoke it again, "I have never ever heard that word, shapeshifter."

"Rhiannon can change form. Before she married Pwyll, she often would roam her special hill in the form of a white horse . . . ."

"But she rode a white horse," again Ophelia broke in.

"Oh, yes, you know the story well! She did ride a white horse, and she could also take the form of a similar white horse, one in the same family, actually. Rhiannon's kinship with the horses is so strong that even to this day, she can still transform herself into the mystical white horse. Once in awhile, she still goes out into the hills and the meadows and rides like the wind."

"I thought that she 'rode like the wind' on the horse!" squealed Ophelia.

"She does that, too, and sometimes, she experiences the ride as the horse. Rhiannon is that connected, and she has the power of shapeshifting."

"Shapeshifting?" asked Ophelia again.

"Yes, and you, too have this power."

"You mean that I can turn into a horse?" Ophelia asked.

"Probably not, although you never know!" replied Artemis. "What I mean is that you have the power to change form. Right now, you are a growing girl. In the next few years, you will be experiencing many changes. So you will be shapeshifting as a natural part of growing up.

"You can also choose to shapeshift. If there is a time when you are not pleased with where you are in your life; if you aren't pleased with who you are in your life—shapeshift. Change it! You can consciously choose, no matter what, to pick yourself up and purposefully evolve more into the girl that you want to be. You, Ophelia, have the power to shapeshift." Artemis looked deep into Ophelia's eyes with that knowing look, which seemed to bestow something upon her.

"This power is not something that anyone else gives you," Artemis spoke, as if she had read Ophelia's thoughts. "It is always there with you. It was there from the moment you were born, and it will remain with you until you are no more. You carry it with you. The power is within you."

"How did I get this power? Was it like when your father, Zeus, gave you the gifts as a girl?"

"No, Ophelia. No one gives it to you. It is already yours."

"How did I get that special?" asked Ophelia, suddenly a bit afraid, wondering if somehow she was like all the other women in these stories. Would she have to carry a heavy burden, like Rhiannon? Would she become a holy woman like Kuan Yin? Would she be responsible for all of nature like Amaterasu? Would she never marry like Artemis? She spoke about these things to Artemis, who looked at the girl with great compassion. Artemis felt a sincere caring and connection to Ophelia, whom she looked upon as a little sister.

"Oh, Ophelia," Artemis gently spoke, "You will carry heavy burdens, although not in the way that Rhiannon did. Every human carries burdens in his or her life—it is a part of life to learn about those burdens—when to carry them, when to set them down, and how to shift them into golden opportunities. Therein is the chance to be the shapeshifter that you are.

"And each one is a holy woman in her own way, for we walk with the spark of something greater than we are, creating through our words and through our acts. You may not enter a hermitage, like Kuan Yin, or dedicate your life to the sacred path—and yet, all paths are sacred. Whatever you do in your life, let it be with the wisdom of the divine, which wishes to express through you. In that way, you shift the situations of the world, elevating them to something better. You are the holy woman, and you are the shapeshifter, for you do not accept things at face value, but see the greater potential held within them.

"As for Amaterasu, you already know that you are connected to all of nature. It is why you love being outside so much. It feeds you on your innermost level. And yes, you have a responsibility for all things in the natural world, whether you accept that responsibility or not. If each of you humans do not claim this necessary responsibility, and act from that place of conscious choice, what will happen? . . . More pollution and devastation of your natural resources. Extinction of valuable animal and plant species, and the collapse of the natural balance. You must take on this one, Ophelia!"

Then, Artemis giggled, "As for getting married, I don't tell the future, but I would imagine that you will have your own family someday."

Artemis reached a hand out to touch Ophelia's leg, as she smiled. "Again, I know not what form that will take, for loving families come in many forms . . . . But you will have one; that I do believe."

The two lingered only a few minutes more, for the moon was rising behind Artemis' head and Ophelia had to get home.

It was this conversation that Ophelia reflected on now, as she remembered Artemis' encouraging words . . . .

Ophelia realized that her body was a part of the natural world and that she couldn't force it to develop faster, any more than she could force open the buds on the rosebush in her mother's garden.

She also realized in this moment that she had the power to shapeshift . . . . Ophelia chose, right then and there, to let go of the taunts from Sara Beth. So what if she didn't have her period yet? She didn't even care about getting it right now. It would come in its own perfect time. Life had a way of doing that.

be gentle
with yourself
you are growing

PATIENCE

Winds of Change

The Nothing That We Are

To listen to or download this song, go to itunes.com

Post-afternoon light,

but pre-twilight;

pale rays shine.

The air isn't warm,

and it's not quite cool,

but still you can feel it.

There's something about the nothing that we are,

there's something about the dull hours that promise us a star.

Before pinks and pastel reds

start fading westward bound,

When numb conversations almost hint towards change,

and breezes hardly sigh.

There's something about the nothing that we are,

there's something about the dull hours that promise us a star.

There's something about the grass when it's brown,

that something will let you know it'll turn green somehow,

somehow... somehow...

There's something about the way you don't know me,

there's something about the way I don't know you.

There's something about the dull hours that promise us a star,

there's something about the nothing that we are...

By Erienne Romaine, written at age 13

Jazz singer/songwriter
The Scenic Route CD
www.erienneromaine.com

Ophelia's Oracle—New Adventures!

Demeter & Persephone—mothers & daughters

Yemaya—friends, the ebb & flow

Ixchel—weaving a greater community, moon cycles

Changing Woman—the beauty in all of your stages

In the next Ophelia's Oracle book, you will meet four new awesome goddesses! Ophelia's journey to find out more about herself and her connections with other girls and their cultures inspires her to learn about four new goddesses. Each of them has a profound influence on Ophelia's life.

Ophelia's relationship with her mom becomes more difficult and emotional as she pushes for more separation and independence. "Sometimes my mom is my best friend, and we have great times together. And then she turns into such a dork that I'm embarrassed to be seen with her."

The classic Greek myth of **Demeter and Persephone** tells the story of the blissful state of a mother and daughter relationship that is changed when Persephone enters the Underworld to learn more about her dark side. Demeter is devastated and doesn't allow crops to grow while Persephone is away. As Ophelia explores this story, she begins to understand the strength of her connection to her mother and why it seems frayed and uncertain at this time.

Through a new friend from Africa, Ophelia learns about **Yemaya**, the Yoruban ocean goddess who represents the natural ebb and flow of female power. "Sometimes I don't say what I think, because I want everyone to like me. I'm afraid to speak up in class because the boys will think I'm trying to be smarter." Ophelia strives more to be liked, to please her classmates, and to hide her outgoing, smart self. With Yemaya at her side, she becomes empowered to be herself, instead of worrying about what others want from her.

Ophelia struggles with changes in her body and the big swings in her moods that make her wonder who she is going to be every day! "Everything was perfect last year. I had friends and I loved my horseback riding. I was good in math and my teacher always praised me. This year sucks. Nothing is the same. Everyone comments on how tall I am. I feel clumsy. And my grades have fallen. I hate my life!" **Changing Woman**, the Navajo and Apache earth mother, goddess of wisdom, teaches Ophelia about the natural flow of changes in a girl's life. Ophelia explores her resistance to change and learns how to embrace it.

When Ophelia gets to visit her father's mother in New Mexico, she is feeling stuck and unable to appreciate her own creativity. "Nothing I do turns out right. It makes me just not want to try new things!" Her grandmother shares the story of **Ixchel**, the moon goddess who spins her creative web and teaches girls to open up to all the new possibilities in their lives. When Ophelia is visited by a dragonfly, another symbol of Ixchel, Ophelia receives a message that takes her in a whole new direction.

Be sure to check out the Ophelia's Oracle web site to find out when her story continues. You can sign up on the web site to be on the mailing list so you will receive notifications of our next release.

www.opheliasoracle.com

Donna and Tina growing into women!

A story from Tina

When I was 11, my Dad took me to the City Pound to pick out a dog. I was so excited—I was finally getting the companion I had wanted for a few years. We walked up and down the aisles looking at the dogs, some who were curled up in a ball, some who looked scared, and some who definitely wanted our attention. I fell in love with a young female German shepherd, and she went home with us that day. Missy became my constant companion, someone I could talk to when I was lonely and play with when I was happy. She always responded in just the right way.

One summer day, I noticed that Missy was holding her mouth really strangely, like she had something inside but wasn't chewing on it. I opened her mouth and reached in and pulled out the tiniest animal, which was all wet, of course. I cuddled it close to me and took it inside and dried it off. My mom and I recognized it as a baby opossum, an animal that lives in its mother's pouch sucking milk until it is large enough to emerge. Even then, the mother opossum keeps the babies with her, carrying them on her back.

We immediately found a doll baby bottle I had and gave the baby opossum some milk and a name, Pogo. She drank greedily and grew very fast. We kept her in a box downstairs. Within a few weeks, she could get out of

Winds of Change

her box, and she would climb the stairs (she was much smaller than a stair) and come into my bedroom. From then on, she followed me everywhere. My mom said that this was called "imprinting," and that a baby animal will become attached to the creature who takes care of it. Pogo thought I was her mother!

She would perch on my shoulder and as she got older would follow after me on the ground. I would take Missy and Pogo into a wooded area near our house to my favorite spot, a tree that had fallen but was resting on some of its branches. I could climb up on it and sit and watch my two best friends, sniffing and exploring their environments. It was then that I knew I wanted to be a biologist. Nothing seemed more interesting to me than understanding how animals interacted with their world.

And many years later, I got a masters degree in wildlife biology, the fulfillment of a dream that started with a dog and a "possum."

For more information, refer to Tina's website at www.tinaproctor.com.

A story from Donna

When I was growing up, I had two separate selves. One part was the girl who was an "A" student, easily made friends, and liked to talk. The other was the girl who held a secret. I tried not to think about that part because that girl was being hurt by some people who my family had asked to take care of me. Instead, they were doing some really bad things physically and sexually. It hurt, and so most of the time I just pretended that it wasn't true. I didn't think that I could tell anyone and make it stop. I had been told that if I did tell, then really bad things would happen to my sister . . . so I just kept the secret, even though it made me very sad.

I now know that it is typical for someone in my situation to act this way. Abusers often tell lies to keep girls quiet. Even though I was a smart girl, I didn't figure it out. If anyone ever hurts you, you need to tell an adult. And if the first person that you tell doesn't help you, then tell someone else.

I learned that no matter what someone does to you, or what they say about you, it does not define who you are. It is never too late to learn to have fun, to appreciate life, and to openly share with others. My life is such a wonderful adventure! I do not let the fact that there was hardship in my young life affect my days now. I believe that there is an opportunity in all experiences, and that we can learn from them. Even hardships can help us grow into the women that we were meant to be!

For more information, refer to Donna's website at www.inlightenedsource.com.

"Each moment slips away
into the forever abyss of yesterday
and falls deeper into the never-ending mystery
of tomorrow."

Madelyn, age 15

Dream your dreams awake

Take a little time to be by yourself and daydream about the stories you have read in this book . . . . Allow your mind to wander to the newness of the rising sun each day (even if you aren't up to see it!) Just like the sun, you can greet the day with expectancy for the possibilities that it brings . . . . Invite the qualities of Amaterasu to join you; carry an understanding of our connection with all living things in the natural world. Perhaps today you will notice the newly fallen snow or the spring buds on the tree. Even a puddle of rain or a bit of mud can hold wonderment if you truly look at it. That curiosity ripples out and exists with all of the people that you meet, too. Each one has value regardless of their outer circumstances. Even when times of disagreement surface, you stretch to recognize what is possible, beyond the discord.

At noontime, you contemplate yourself, noticing any points of insecurity or doubt and reaffirming what YOU know to be true about who you are and what you are learning and doing in the world. You draw to you the people who support your innermost vision of yourself and who build you up, rather than those who tear you down. You allow your spirit to roam free, riding on the wind like Rhiannon.

In the evening, you move gracefully into the supportive embrace of Kuan Yin, who is a constant reminder of the need to ground your purest intentions into the physical world through your own unique path of service. Kuan Yin reminds you to be gentle and to have compassion with everyone, including yourself.

As night sets in, and the moon begins to rise, Artemis is steadfast as your guardian while you embrace sweet sleep. She gifts you a confident sense of inner and outer protection . . . . You rest and dream of bold adventures that only a girl like you can imagine. Artemis trusts that you possess all that you need in your personal "backpack," and that you draw in extra support from others, too. Grandmother Moon smiles upon you and enlivens your innermost destiny, illuminating your path with a beautiful warm glow.

Life is good. You are precious.
You have much to give, and you will make a difference in the world.
Thank you for being—you!

Final Inspiration

Women have been inspired by the stories in this book for hundreds of years. They represent parts of the divine feminine that are within you. What does this mean? You are a goddess! You have the thread of history behind you and the brightness of the future ahead of you. Know that who you are now is exactly who you need to be. Celebrate your beautiful, evolving self!

Postscript

In 2001, when we began this book project, I asked to be guided to be in alignment with my truest intention. That intention was to reach a welcoming hand to the younger ones, guiding them in the "old way," so that the journey might be a little softer and a little richer.

This is the center through which we birthed this book. We truly felt the presence of the women of the ages—both those who lived and those of myths and legends—guiding us, assisting us. We felt a destiny unfolding. And we both felt a determined commitment to see this project through in a way which was deeply meaningful. We had a full commitment to it; it became more than just a book.

As the information was inspired through us, it was as if what we had to say would make a difference, not only to the girls, but also to other women. We often heard, "I wish I had had that kind of thing when I was growing up! My mother and I were never close." And even for those of us who had a close and loving relationship with our mothers, our aunts, or our grandmothers, how many of us were raised in the "old way" of mother and grandmother passing on the feminine wisdom? It is not that we were neglected or abused necessarily. Just that somewhere during our collective evolution, the path to the fountain was forgotten, and the sweet nectar of women's ancient wisdom was lost. That wisdom is pushing to return, so we might bring balance within ourselves, our families, our countries, and the world.

If what Tina and I have shared in these pages reaches one girl, and speaks to her in her heart of hearts, then we have done something worthwhile. For that understanding and that confidence will ripple onward and reach others through that one girl. And one to one, heart to heart, the word will be shared, and changes will be made, as it is the old way of woman to make a difference, and to bring forth the healing in a quiet, yet powerful wave, through a sisterhood connection.

The wisdom of the ages is available to us! I have been truly inspired and blessed by this project over its eight years in development. Now I offer it, with gratitude, to all who have spoken through me . . . .

Donna

July 2009

Winds of Change

Artists' Notes

Sue Lion

One thing I really love about drawing is I can put lots of symbolism in each image, sometimes a little hidden at first glance. Take a look at Ophelia and each of the goddesses below and try to find all the of the symbols. I've listed some of them, but because every person sees art in a different way, there may be others you find that are important to you.

Ophelia – Inner Wisdom

Ophelia is dancing with the music of the universe knowing that she is embraced and protected by Mother Earth.

- Ophelia is joyously dancing on **Mother Earth's loving hand.**
- **The spiral** draws the power of the universe to Ophelia's core, her heart. Then, when she is filled up, she can, in turn, radiate her love back to those she can touch.
- Do you see that the trees are changing into the **butterfly**? Butterfly energy is about transformation, something Ophelia is experiencing every day.
- **The Milky Way** reminds us that we are surrounded by amazing beauty and astounding possibilities. All we have to do is pay attention.

Amaterasu – Beauty

By carrying the light in her heart, Amaterasu becomes beautiful in every way and lets her light shine on everyone.

- **An eight-sided mirror** reflects the light of her sun back to her heart.
- **A cave** is dark but holds the promise of light when the door is open.
- **Weaving** is an important art in Japanese culture and in this drawing the stalks of **rice** are woven together to highlight both the rice and weaving.
- **Water** represents the deepest emotions and intuition we have. Amaterasu learned to trust her inner emotions and to let her light shine.

Rhiannon – Trust

Rhiannon believes that the cruel things said about her are true. When her son is returned to her, she learns to trust her intuition.

- Rhiannon has a **magical ability to ride a powerful horse or BE that powerful horse.** In this drawing, she and the horse are together but separate.
- Rhiannon's desire to **hold her baby** never leaves her. In this drawing, her arm is holding her son, even though he is in another kingdom for awhile.
- The wide expanse of **farmland** separated Rhiannon and Pwyll from their son but because of the honesty of the lord and lady in the neighboring kingdom, Rhiannon's son was returned.

Kuan Yin – Compassion

With true compassion, Kuan Yin teaches us that with patience, we can accomplish our heart's desire.

- **Water** is the place of our deepest intuition and feelings. Not only does Kuan Yin pour water on the fire but she stands on water as well.
- The **water vessel** holds an abundance of energy that can put out a fire in the face of adversity.
- **Lotus blossoms** show us pure love and embody our connection to a higher power.
- **Fire** can symbolize anger and fear, and either can be destructive. But fire can also be the passion for what we do.
- **Sunlight** lights the way. The reflection of light is a reminder to let our feelings and intuition take us from a place of fear into a place of light.
- The **white tiger** carries us to a safe place and stands guard to keep us safe.

Artemis – Strength

Artemis represents the strength we bring to our own lives as we protect and nurture those around us.

- **Artemis's bow** is the shape of the moon. The moon illuminates the darkness and represents the powerful, feminine, nuturing force.
- **Songbirds** (in the trees) represent the underlying music that surrounds us all the time if we take the time to quiet our minds, turn off our computers and cell phones, and listen to the songs of the earth.

- All living creatures have special attributes: **Fireweed** – Growth, **Butterfly** – Transformation, **Bear** – Introspection, **Wolf** – Spirit teacher, **Mountain lion** – Leadership, powerful self, **Deer** – Gentleness, **Eagle** – Illumination, **Morning glory** – Opens its fresh face with the dawn, the beginning of all new things

Crossing the Threshold

Now you are ready to cross the threshold of adventure and see life as powerful and beautiful.

- **Two lovely tree spirits** sway in the gentleness of life, branches entwined in friendship.
- **Trees** connect us with the nurturing of Mother Earth and the grandeur of the sky.
- **Wind** gently stirs imaginations to great heights.
- Birds live in the immense space of air: **Raven**, unafraid of the darkness, brings healing power to those who need it; **Falcon** happily carries the messages from the universe to us; **Songbird** (in the shadows of the trees) brings music to us whenever we are willing listen.

A little about myself

Having been a closet artist all my early life, I finally took my first official art class, basic drawing, in college while majoring in physical education. I loved the class so much, I changed my lifelong career to art. I've never regretted it.

Colored pencils and ink have always intrigued me. I can take them with me, even snowshoeing or hiking in the mountains, with little fuss. I add my original poetry to my drawings to add depth to the message. Look for some hidden symbolism in each drawing – a fun way to add surprise and lightheartedness.

Living next to open space in Colorado has made it possible for me to take in the color, tone, and mystery of nature. Great horned owls, coyotes, foxes, deer, and bobcats have crossed my deck and my energy field and I breathe in the magic to bring it forth again in my drawings.

www.suelionink.com

Go to www.opheliasoracle.com, for upcoming workshops for girls who want to contribute their art to future books in our series.

Rachelle Donahoe

Seven whimsical drawings in this book were created by Rachelle Donahoe, a gifted inspirational artist. Rachelle says:

It all started in 1999 when I bought a set of Prismacolor markers. I had never drawn in this style before, and all of a sudden, all of these words and images began pouring out of me. I began creating work to remind myself of lessons I wanted to learn or to process something I was going through. I still call them my "notes to myself."

free your mind • open your heart

I love the idea of surrounding myself with uplifting and inspiring messages—and I love the idea of sharing them even more, because I believe my purpose is to celebrate my wholeness as a woman and to use my creativity and love to inspire, empower, and transform the world.

Many Blessings,

Rachelle

Rachelle's illustrations are available as greeting cards, prints, and magnets at www.rachelleart.com

A heartfelt sharing of ancient feminine wisdom,

a timeless understanding,

the comfort and support that every girl

(and woman) craves,

to welcome her to her fullest potential.

Portals of Pride

Ophelia's Oracle includes five Portals of Pride – crossing each threshold is significant to every girl's positive development.

In the *Heart of the Goddess*, Hallie Inglehart Austen says, "What does the Goddess represent to us at this point in time? She is love combined with power, creating the potential for a more powerful love and a more loving power."

The decision to call the sections "Portals of Pride" was an inspired, yet conscious choice. In times past, pride was considered a negative, even "sinful" trait. In this present day, we are learning how to possess the assurance of knowing ourselves and believing in ourselves, and having our actions stem from that awareness. Strong, boasting, self-centered pride is *still* not to be desired! A gentle confidence in oneself, which also acknowledges the value and contribution of others, is a balanced and grounded place from which excellence can express.

Pride is a helpful ingredient to success these days—the ability to feel pleased at a job well done, to be inwardly encouraged to do more, and most importantly to know one's intrinsic value beyond any one achievement. We need to know our core value as individuals. In that way, we can also know our collective worth. We are not threatened by each other because no one else gives us our self-worth, nor diminishes it with their actions. It is from this balanced place of centered worthiness that we can move forward and become more than we have ever been. It is with a healthy sense of pride that we can take personal responsibility to elevate this existence to more than we have ever seen. With a strong, resilient center, we can step into a "more powerful love and a more loving power."

Authors' Bios

Donna DeNomme is an author, speaker, teacher, and ceremonial leader. Having come from a background of brutal abuse, Donna believes there is purpose in all of our experiences. She is the author of *Turtle Wisdom: Coming Home to Yourself*, Finalist Best Books 2007, and Mom's Choice Award 2009 and has been published in the *We Moon Calendar* and in *Talking to Goddess*. Donna loves to witness

the wonder of women and girls coming together for healing and celebration.

Tina Proctor is a biologist, peace advocate, and storyteller, who has spent the past 12 years introducing women and girls to goddess stories from around the world. She has an MS in Wildlife Biology and an MA in Women's Spirituality and has been published in the on-line journal, *Metaformia* and in *Talking to Goddess*, an anthology by D'vorah J. Grenn, PhD. Tina and her husband, Dennis Grogan, have led a long-running Peace Circle, and are trained labyrinth facilitators.